THE
Christmas
CHAPEL

BOOKS BY BARBARA JOHNSON WITCHER

NON-FICTION

*Create the Job You Love and
Make Plenty of Money*

Part-Time Jobs for Full-Time Mothers

FICTION

Heirs of Abraham

The Christmas Chapel

THE

Christmas

CHAPEL

— ◆ ◆ ◆ —

Barbara Johnson Witcher

WESTBOW
PRESS
A DIVISION OF THOMAS NELSON

WestBow Press books may be ordered through booksellers or by contacting:

WestBow Press
A Division of Thomas Nelson
1663 Liberty Drive
Bloomington, IN 47403
www.westbowpress.com
1-(866) 928-1240

ISBN: 978-1-4908-0599-3 (sc)
ISBN: 978-1-4908-0600-6 (hc)
ISBN: 978-1-4908-0598-6 (e)

Library of Congress Control Number: 2013915121

Printed in the United States of America.

WestBow Press rev. date: 8/27/2013

In Acknowledgment

No writer is an island unto herself and certainly this one is not.

In recalling my love of writing, which started when I was six with my first book, "Chippy The Chipmunk", I must thank my mother—Margaret Johnson Menkus—for always encouraging me.

Thanks also to my children, Linda, Laurie and Paul, who grew up watching me scribble on a notepad, put up with my frequent inattention and loved me anyway. Hopefully "kids", you'll enjoy these results.

Thanks to my writer's group. Without Ann Fetter, Cindy Johnson, Lisa Keck, Diana Kightlinger, Darlene Manion, Jeff Norberg and Clyde San Juan, this book wouldn't exist.

Thank you doesn't begin to cover my affection and gratitude for my dear friend and mentor Lois Hudson. Your gentle love and wisdom mean everything.

A special thanks to the cover designer, my first granddaughter Madalyn Marie Worthington. Just as your birth, after all those grandsons, made your Grandpa and I giddy, so your fabulous talent awes me. I'm so proud and glad you're part of this.

I must thank all my family for their love that reminds me of how blessed I am. To my brother Gary Johnson and his Cindy; nephews Jeff and Greg and niece Kelly; grandchildren (besides Madalyn) Michael and Greg Argeros, Katrina and Jeff Mann, Lindsey, Arielle, Melissa, Severina Worthington, Nicole, Rachel and Cade Miller; my first great grandchild, Bradley Mann and the other "children" my own gave me—Severio Worthington, John Sweeney and Gloria Louis Miller—I love you all. And lest I suffer from an empty lap, love to my spoiled dogs, Bucky and Bambi and my fussy felines, Tuxedo and D'Chelle.

Though listed last, always first, THANK YOU GOD for making all this possible.

THE CHRISTMAS CHAPEL DEDICATION:

For my beloved son, Paul Miller and the "daughter" he gave me, his wonderful wife Gloria. This book is about lives changing and through your teaching, Christian walk and beautiful parenting, you change lives for the better every day. That I'm proud of you is an understatement, that I greatly love you is a well known and deserved fact.

DECEMBER 23

CHAPTER I

The Chapel

Benjamin Dickerson's arthritic legs ached as he shuffled on the snow-covered sidewalk. His effort to clear a small path to the chapel, which he had just opened, seemed useless as the blizzard kept pounding down, its snowflakes like tiny bombs heading for hapless targets. Bundled up in a heavy coat, wool earmuffs that pinched the stud earring in his left ear, and tall boots, he could barely remain upright against the onslaught.

The storm had begun the night before, and today it was more relentless. A vicious wind was blowing snow onto the city so rapidly that New Stockford was paralyzed in icy walls of white. Planes could neither leave nor land, and few vehicles could move because the snowplows were impotent on the thickly covered streets.

Benjamin—always called Old Ben even when he was young—shook his head and rubbed the snowflakes from his eyes. Heaving the shovel over his shoulder, he turned back toward the little chapel. It was hopeless to try to clear the sidewalks. He shrugged.

Now that he had done it, he wondered if he had been crazy to even open the small church.

It had been closed since the last part-time minister and the rest of the parishioners had left over two years ago. But tonight he felt, as its caretaker, that it needed to offer shelter to anyone who was caught in the storm. Besides, if it was open again, even just for one night, maybe he could relive the good old days when it was one of the most prestigious buildings on what had once been elegant DeLancey Street. Now, over one hundred years old, the chapel was a fragile, old-fashioned structure that was surrounded by other obsolete, decaying buildings. Almost invisible, it looked to Ben like an old man who had outlived his usefulness.

"Like me?" he whispered to himself.

Dusty gray where its frame used to be white, the church was a sad reminder of a vital community. Once, families of blue-collar workers, suit-coated executives, and Levi-clad academicians filled it with energy and love. Now those residents were all gone, having died off or moved to the suburbs. What they left behind was a forlorn, four-block neighborhood of empty Victorian houses and buildings. While the city hadn't officially started turning dear old DeLancey Street into an industrial section of small factories, he knew that when they did, it would ruin the once proud character of the old street that had been among the city's first settlements. But City Hall didn't seem to care about its historic value. All they wanted was to collect more taxes. And since DeLancey Street was next to the busy downtown district, it was prime property.

"Before long there won't be nothin' left of the ol' times," Ben muttered as he watched the snow blanket the buildings around the tiny church. He glanced across the street where a boarded-up, three-story Victorian stood.

Old Ben sighed. He had lived all his life on DeLancey Street. Though his family's small house had been torn down thirty years ago to make room for a now abandoned motel, he had spent much of his childhood in that big, beautiful house. Miss Emily, who owned it, had entertained not only her own eight children and their friends, but the neighborhood kids as well. There were always a lot of holiday parties, but the after-school cookies and weekly Bible studies were even more special. The house that had once rocked with so much energy and life was now as dead as Miss Emily, who had died in it three years ago.

Ben had heard that a manufacturer was thinking of buying the house and demolishing it to build a glue factory there. *Glue! What a thing to do to that pretty ol' house!* He shook his head and started to trudge back to the chapel's entrance. The snow fell faster now, pounding at him with a fury even more zealous.

Behind him drivers, with their horns blaring, were stalled in their cars. The snow-laden sidewalks were full of people. Desperate to get to their dry, warm destinations, they lowered their heads and plunged through the storm like bulls attacking matadors.

Old Ben threw them a sympathetic look and then turned his attention to the steeple. Though it was barely visible in this storm, he could still make out its illuminated outline. The blue lights of its tall cross were shining beacons in the white-speckled night.

He fought the wind to open the church's front door and hurriedly stepped into the foyer. Stomping the snow off his boots, he hid the shovel in a corner and shrugged out of his heavy coat. He then went to the thermostat and turned up the heat. If people should come tonight, they would need plenty of warmth. And he would give it to them.

Old Ben laughed softly. The trustees would have a fit if they knew what he was doing. But by the time they got the gas and electric bills, it would all be over. Besides, this was probably the last Christmas the little chapel would be here and he would be able to continue living in its back two rooms to care for and protect the place. The trustees were considering selling the church to the developer who would tear it down and sell the land to some stinky factory. The thought sickened him.

He ran stubby fingers through his thick, gray crew cut. This was not a night to be thinking about the chapel's demise. This was a night to be hospitable if indeed that was what God needed him and the chapel to be.

Normally, he would have spent this December 23 like he usually did, by himself with his DVD banjo lessons and paperback Western novels. Since he had retired eight years ago and his Nellie had died four Christmases ago, there really wasn't anything else for him to do. They had never been gifted with children, and the few nieces and nephews they'd once known had scattered. So he was all alone—a hermit who had started talking to himself but was struggling to keep from answering his own solitary comments.

"Don't start answering yourself," someone had once warned him, "because that's a sure sign you're going crazy!"

He sure didn't want that! To be known as Crazy Old Ben would be just awful. It was bad enough being known as Old Ben. He grinned. "Though I guess at seventy-three I do fit the description," he said to the chapel as he pushed open the swinging doors that led to the sanctuary.

He unbuttoned his thick, blue cardigan. The heat hugged him as he flicked on the overhead lights that chased away the dusk's darkness. He watched with satisfaction as they bathed the oak-paneled walls with a golden sheen that added sparkle to the stained-glass windows that were set in them. There were eight, created to portray the life of Christ by a long-forgotten parishioner over eighty years ago.

Old Ben looked at the left wall first. Those four glass portrayals were his favorites, showing the nativity scene with the wise men and shepherds; Jesus as a boy in the temple being confronted by his worried parents; Jesus being baptized by John the Baptist; and Jesus healing the sick.

He shifted his gaze to the right and an automatic frown

dented his already lined face. These were the pictures he didn't like because they showed the suffering of his beloved Lord. There were scenes of Jesus praying in the garden of Gethsemane; of him carrying his cross through an angry mob; of him being crucified on that cross in the midst of thieves. Only the last one was easy to bear, as it was of Jesus standing by his empty tomb, talking to Mary Magdalene. That was the one that showed he had risen from the dead. Even though Old Ben understood the necessity for the tragic death, he always felt bad that it had happened to a nice guy like Jesus.

"But tonight we're thinkin' 'bout the baby," he said to the pictures as he walked to the front where earlier he had dragged the big boxes out of storage and reverently unpacked the four-foot-tall nativity scene. He dusted off the ceramic figures and placed them in the center of the raised altar. The huge mahogany cross soared above the scene as if reaching into heaven itself. In years past, they always had a Christmas tree decorated with white doves and blue lights, but Old Ben had not thought to get one. In fact he had not thought to decorate the little chapel at all until the weather had turned so bad. Somehow, deep within his being, he felt an overwhelming need to open up the place and make it look again like the haven of safety, warmth, and celebration that it used to be.

He went to the front pew and rubbed his gnarled hands over the smooth, well-worn wood. This was the pew that he and his wife had always sat in when the church was full. A shy smile crossed his face. "If only for tonight," he said to the chapel, "you'll be yourself again. And if no one comes to spend time with you, well … me and my Nellie'll be here."

The thought of his wife twisted his heart, and tears sprung to his eyes.

Old Ben looked at the altar and remembered, as though it was yesterday, how he had stood there. That was a long time ago, and he'd been just a skinny young guy, newly back from the war. As he watched the most beautiful bride in the world walk toward him, he knew he was the luckiest man on earth.

How lovely my Nellie was! We had our whole life ahead of us then. Full of so many hopes and dreams. Those hopes and dreams included a house full of children, but God never blessed them with any. While deeply disappointed, they never lost their love for the Lord, and so they gave their energy and devotion to this church—DeLancey Street Community—and to the many children who first learned about Jesus there.

How his wife had loved to put on the kids' programs, cook for the suppers, make pies for the bake sales and quilts for the poor. He nodded proudly. His Nellie was a regular workaholic when it came to serving the church. And he was right there with her—repairing and building anything and everything.

He looked up at the giant wooden cross that he had built. "What am I gonna do without you? You're all I have now."

He rubbed his forehead to erase his worry about the future and moved firmly over to the small mahogany organ at the side of the altar. Turning it on was the last thing he had to do to restore the chapel to its former glory. He pushed a few buttons and turned on the automatic music that had long ago been preprogrammed to play fifteen of the most beloved Christmas hymns that members of the church, and especially the children, used to sing with such enthusiastic gusto.

Satisfied that he had returned the chapel to what it used to be, he started to move back to the front pew. Suddenly the outer door scraped open and he blinked with joyful surprise. It sounded like people were coming in. The blue steeple lights must have attracted them, even if the sidewalks he tried to clear were still full of snow. He knew that once they got inside, they would find warmth—and peace.

He looked back at the baby in the manger and beamed. *We're gonna have us some company Lil' Jesus! We're gonna have us some company!*

CHAPTER 2

The Frustrated Businessman

Adam Blake stepped into the simple chapel. A tall man, his every move exuded the power and confidence that it took to build a multi-billion dollar empire. Clearly, he was not someone who could suffer even the slightest inconvenience, mainly because his life was constantly controlled by clocks. Now the small one on his Omega wristwatch proclaimed it to be six in the evening. If it wasn't for the blasted snowstorm, he would be home behind his gated community of multi-million dollar homes in New Stockford Heights. Instead he was here in this wretched neighborhood that was almost a slum.

With a quick, purposeful stride, he took a seat in the back pew and assessed his surroundings. He shook his head and looked at the carpet under his cold, wet feet. It was a deep maroon and threadbare in spots. Wiggling in the hard seat, he studied the high walls that reached to the arched ceiling, noticing small cobwebs that clung to the top of them. A corner of his mouth lifted. Most certainly none of the others who were coming into this God forsaken place would notice those. But everybody who knew him even slightly could attest that he noticed every detail, especially if it smacked of imperfection.

Adam watched as people trudged in. He could tell that they were from disparate social classes and, like him, had not been able to go anywhere in this blizzard. But that, he was certain, would be all they had in common. Except of course that most of them surely consumed some of what his many companies manufactured. He supposed that meant that they contributed to his extraordinary personal income. But that did not mean that he had to interact with them—to make small talk until the storm went away. He stiffened his shoulders and pressed them tightly to his sides, as though attempting to shut the people out of his space. No! Adam Blake never just chatted with anyone unless they were in a position to add to the success that made him more money.

Reaching into the pocket of his cashmere overcoat, his face creased. His cell was in the car along with his briefcase. He massaged his brow and felt its deep lines. It was no wonder he couldn't remember them. That blasted phone call had been so unnerving that it practically paralyzed his brain.

Once again he looked around the room. His gaze briefly stopped at the stained glass windows and the cross and nativity scene at the altar.

"When was the last time I stepped foot in a church?" he asked himself. "Probably when Bobby was baptized. Twenty-five years ago. And that was a real church. Not a poor excuse like this."

A vision crossed his mind of the large brick building that housed his place of worship. It was the most prestigious church in the affluent suburb where he lived. Belonging to the King Cathedral was almost as impressive as belonging to the Eagle Ridge Country Club. That church was supposed to be a house of God, open to anyone who chose to worship there. But the truth was that like its social counterpart, no one really belonged who didn't have incomes of six and preferably seven figures. In fact, both the church and country club were snobbishly intimidating. Especially the King Cathedral. In spite of its wealthy façade, it seemed to always be in a financial crisis.

That place costs me a fortune. And Marilyn happily pays it.

His heart knotted at the thought of his wife. Even after three decades of marriage and when most of his friends had young, trophy wives to display on their arms, he still considered Marilyn the perfect mate for him. Involved with several charities, she gave him the public persona of being a great benefactor. Secretly he couldn't be bothered with caring for people other than his immediate family. That was Marilyn's department and she spent his money lavishly. He didn't care. He could more than afford the donations, which also gave him much needed tax breaks.

Most important of all, it pleased him that he'd become so successful that he and his wife were important members of the high society set. Doers and shakers in a town where most of his neighbors came from family money that reached back to beyond the founding of the country. Many even had European titles. Though Adam rubbed elbows with them at the club's social events, they were not his friends.

He knew the reason he discouraged even the most sincere overtures of friendship. It was his secret past. The one he had so carefully hidden. He knew that if he ever allowed himself to get close to those Barons, Earls and Trust Fund Blue Bloods, he might slip and betray his peasant roots. And then everyone would know what a fraud he really was. So while he was always polite with impeccable manners, he kept a civilized social distance, claiming colossal business pressures that made the time it would take for friendships impossible. That was certainly true. He made the money and his wife spent it.

Marilyn gave Adam's money and her time to several organizations, King's Cathedral most of all, which included dragging the kids to Sunday school almost every Sunday. But Adam begged off attending services even at Christmas and

Easter, because he was just too busy giving them the good life. One much better than he had ever had.

Leaning forward in the pew, he stared at his alligator shoes now soaked with snow. There was a thousand dollars ruined. Not that such a paltry sum would matter to him one way or the other. But it was the principle of the thing. And the fact that now he would have to take some time to replace them.

When he walked out of his office to his Bentley in its special spot in the underground garage of the thirty-story building that was his corporation's headquarters, he hadn't expected to get even slightly wet. Of course he knew he was going out in the storm. But the car had cost a fortune and it was expected to be reliable and run no matter what. Instead it let him down and stalled after barely moving half a mile.

He rubbed his still brown hair that a weekly trim kept perfect and wiggled his icy toes in his soggy shoes. Both the car and shoes were useless. A complete waste of money!

The room grew warm as people continued filling it. He took off his coat and picked at the crease of his silk suit pants. He knew that what Marilyn said was true. That all he thought about was money.

He sighed. It was easy for his wife to say since she knew nothing about what it was like to be poor. A pain started its dull tapping inside his head and he shoved fingers into his eyes, kneading them roughly. If she had grown up like him she would understand and appreciate all that he gave to her and their spoiled rotten kids.

He buried his face in his hands. Usually the new life he had created for himself was enough to keep the painful thoughts away. But since the afternoon's phone call, they were again wrapping their long tentacles around his soul, squeezing out the little joy he had and reminding him of things he had never dared tell even his wife.

He had been just six years old on the day that his father left him. Even now, fifty years later, he remembered every sordid detail as though it had happened a mere hour ago.

He was playing in a dirt yard in front of a rundown duplex apartment with his little brother Joey. The only toy they had was an old basketball. It had lost some of its air but they were throwing, kicking and rolling it as if it were the most wonderful thing in the world, while inside their apartment their parents' angry voices assaulted them. Even at six, Adam knew that the words his Mom and Dad were screaming at each other were terribly cruel and maybe even unforgivable. Joey, who was a year younger, put his thumb in his mouth as he often did when he was frightened.

Adam had just put an arm around his brother's skinny shoulders and was attempting to stop the thumb sucking when his father burst out of the apartment with a big suitcase in his hand. He grabbed his father's arm as he tried to hurry past them. "Where are you going Daddy? Can I go with you?"

Hal Blake hesitated and tousled the top of his son's hair. "No son. No you can't." His gray eyes were soft and his lips wrinkled sadly. "I'm sorry." Then he turned and rushed to his car without looking back as his wife's shrill epithets followed him.

Gunning the motor, he sped away while his sons solemnly clung to each other, watching him. Jagged tears made light lines on their dirty faces.

When Hal's car was out of sight, their mother, Millie, opened the door. A cigarette hung from a corner of her wide mouth and a tall, full glass of brown liquid was in her right hand. She braced herself against the doorframe. "You boys get in here. Right now!"

Joey had started crying loudly and she glared at him. "Shut up!" She turned to Adam. "Take care of your brother. Make him stop that bellowing. You know I can't stand it. Gives me a headache."

Without a word, Adam lifted his brother, who was almost

as big as he was. He carried him into the house and into their small bedroom. They didn't leave it until night and they were so hungry that they were forced to bother their mother.

"Mama?" Adam asked quietly. "We're hungry." Millie's eyes were half closed as she lay on the sofa. He moved close to her and gently touched her arm. "Mama? Can we have something to eat?"

She swayed as she forced herself to sit up. "Don't bother me!" she yelled as she slapped him. Then she looked around her. "Where's my drink? I need my drink."

Adam picked up the glass from the floor where it was lying on its side and handed it to her.

She glared at it, then at him. "You spilled my drink. You bad boy." She hit him again.

"No Mama. No I didn't." He pointed to the floor as Joey, with his thumb firmly in his mouth, started to cry. "I found it on the floor. It was already spilled."

His mother hugged the glass to her. "Go away! Leave me alone. You're bad boys. Just like your father." Then she screamed the same words at them that she had used at her husband.

Quickly Adam took Joey into the kitchen. All they could find was some stale bread and mayonnaise, which they ate with water before hurrying back to their room where they huddled together on a small cot to hide from their mother.

They never saw or heard from their father again. Soon Millie went on welfare, using much of the state's money on liquor and cigarettes. Eventually, she became so dysfunctional that the legal system took her boys from her. She didn't seem to care.

Adam winced with cynicism. *Joey and I ended up in a bunch of foster homes where we were supposed to be better off!*

The first one the boys were placed in worked them to death and hardly fed them. The house was full of heavy antique furniture that Joey had to dust, his little fingers fitting perfectly into the carved wood. Adam had to scrub and polish the wooden floors on his hands and knees plus clean the kitchen. Other children, who were all wards of the state, had similar chores. While the foster parents ate meat and vegetables, their charges were given only bread, gravy and a few vegetables.

Their next home, which they were sent to when seven-year-old Joey started stealing the people's cigarettes and liquor so he could sell them, was a little better. At least those foster parents fed them decently. They had to work there too but it wasn't as bad. Yet those so called parents were mean too, not using any of the boys' support money for them. Any clothes they wore were given to them by people in their church. When they got them they were already old, stained and often ripped. Adam cringed at the memory of how they forced them to go to church in those awful clothes that the other kids had thrown away and could identify. How he hated the humiliating embarrassment. Then there was Christmas when the welfare people would give the couple gifts for their foster children. But they gave them to their own kids instead and all Adam and his brother got was one orange they had to share. This, for them, was a wonderful treat.

Now, smoothing the front of his custom-made suit coat, he scowled. "We always looked like little bums," he said to himself. "No wonder I'm such a clotheshorse now. I'm making up for what I didn't have."

As a kid, Adam was shy but he forced himself to be obedient, helpful and a good student. Joey, however, was very different. Inside him was such bitterness at what life had dealt them that he rebelled, fighting anyone and anything that represented the system. Petty thefts, knife fights and drug dealing had all landed him in Juvenile Hall.

After Joey was taken away and Adam was eleven, he was placed with Stella Markowitz and her brother Peter. Neither had married and since Peter had become wealthy as the owner of a candy company, they had decided to share their good fortune with foster children. They encouraged Adam and the two girls they were also fostering to concentrate on school. Adam was only too eager to oblige.

Settling in with the Markowitzes, Adam became the perfect kid. He never saw his brother again and eventually his sadness over him lessened. The reason he could get over Joey and his miserable past was because Adam had grown to love his new foster parents, who he called Uncle Pete and Aunt Stella. They returned his love, buying him every new edition of the action hero comic books he still collected today. Uncle Pete even paid for his Harvard education and when Adam graduated, he took him into his candy company.

"I'm a confirmed bachelor," the rotund Markowitz said as he led Adam to the private office with Adam's name freshly painted on the door. "So you've become the son I never had. And someday this will all be yours." His eyes twinkled. "If you work hard and allow me to guide you. Like a good son should," he added, his round belly bouncing with laughter. The arrangement had been fine at first. Uncle Pete taught Adam everything he knew. He even trusted him with his secret chocolate caramel bar recipe that had made him rich.

Through his new Ivy League acquaintances, Adam discovered the importance of the right image and pedigree, which meant doing what he could to avoid being embarrassed by his foster family. Whenever Adam met anyone not associated with Stella and Peter, he gave them an invented story about his early life.

I told everybody how my well-educated parents had died in an automobile accident when I was little. Since there had been no one else to take me in, a distant cousin of my mother's, who was a simple person, raised me. That's how I explained my foster parents to the few who met them.

Adam's "Uncle Pete" might have been successful and rich but deep down he was really just a blue-collar worker in an ill-fitting suit. And in spite of all his goodness, Adam was ashamed of him. Yet as much as he disdained Uncle Pete's plain ways, he had still taken the job, title, private office and money that the old man provided while always on the lookout for something better.

Because I vowed never to be poor, dirty or hungry again. And to do whatever it took to make sure that would never happen.

A better opportunity came four years later. He had been dating Marilyn Johnson, a debutante he'd met through one of his Harvard classmates. She appealed to him on many levels. First and of course most obvious, she was beautiful. Her red hair, green eyes and slender figure exuded class no matter what she wore. She was also bright, articulate and kind. Her kindness, especially, appealed to him. Probably because he had lived so much of his life in an unkind world. But there was still another reason why Adam found Marilyn so appealing. Her father was the leading cookie manufacturer in the country. And Mr. Johnson was everything he wanted to be.

Because of his fabricated history, Adam realized that he could never dare introduce Marilyn to Uncle Pete and Aunt Stella. Instead he told her that he was just an employee at Markowitz Candy who had worked hard to earn a top position there. And innocent that she was, she accepted that explanation.

When he asked her to marry him and she accepted, Adam knew that if he was to be worthy of Marilyn and the life her family would give him, he would have to have a special meeting with Uncle Pete.

He knew exactly how to manipulate his benefactor. "Uncle Pete," he said as he and the old man were having their usual Monday morning breakfast together. "For years I've been asking you for more responsibility. And you keep telling me no." He looked down at his scrambled eggs with what he hoped was a remorseful expression. "Frankly I don't think you trust me."

Peter wiped a spot of egg yolk from his tie and shook his head. "You know that's not true. I have trusted you with everything. And you run the marketing department. I've even given you the title of Vice President." He wagged a pudgy finger at the young man and grinned. "But my boy, what you want I am not ready to give you. And that's my job. No!" He laughed and his thick white hair, always unruly, flopped wildly. "I am still going to be the head of Markowitz Candy. Until I die that is. Then, it will all be yours."

Adam's jaw quivered tightly as he remembered his future father-in-law's words, given to him just two nights ago. "I'd like you to start a candy division for me," Mr. Johnson said. "Candy and cookies go well together and I think you and I can build quite a dynasty. Especially with what you know from old Markowitz."

So Adam told the old man that he had a good offer from Johnson Cookies. He explained that it had come out of the blue and to his surprise, Markowitz bought his story, probably because he didn't know about Adam's intimate connections with Johnson through Marilyn.

Even after all these years, Adam's heart still ached whenever he thought about that day when he had lost so much more than a job. While he knew Uncle Pete wouldn't promote him, he didn't really expect him to be so kind about letting him go. But all he did was reach over and pat Adam's hand. "My dear boy I will not stand in your way. Go to Johnson. He is bigger than me—and richer. He can offer you a better future than I can."

Though he had orchestrated it, Adam was still devastated at the old man's quick dismissal. It was like being abandoned all over again by his father. And he quickly got back at him by taking Markowitz's secret candy bar recipe over to his new company. He changed it slightly so that it wouldn't invite a lawsuit, and proceeded to take a big share of the nation's candy sales away from his old benefactor.

More often than he wished, Adam allowed himself to think about his deceitful betrayal of his mentor. Then guilt, as heavy as an anvil, weighed him down. But he didn't permit it to last long. Straightening himself up, he reminded his guilty conscience that it was just business - pure and simple. *Besides, everybody who's anybody does whatever it takes to be successful. To make money. To be somebody.*

The years flew by and when his father-in-law died suddenly, he took over the company and ended up as head of a conglomeration that manufactured not just candy and cookies but beverages, pet food, canned meats and frozen dinners. He became one of the richest men not just in America but in the world. And his brother remained a bum.

I always knew Joey was no good. And I was right. Ended up in prison five years ago for robbing a bank at gunpoint. Stupid fool!

Adam had ignored the sensational trial and his brother's sentence as though it had happened to a stranger reported about in the newspapers and on television. Marilyn, however, had followed it. "This bank robber on trial," she teased, "has our last name. Sure he's not a shirt tail relation of yours?"

He had forced a laugh while his stomach knotted. "Not that I know of. Blake's a pretty ordinary name. Must be millions of us. All strangers. Besides," he grew serious, "you know I was an only child."

His eyes burned from the headache still throbbing behind them and he winced as he peered at the stained glass picture of Christ hanging on the cross between two criminals. Then he quickly closed his eyes and sighed. *I'm not my brother's keeper. I don't owe him anything. Especially since he's nothing but a no good bum!*

Which was what he had told the prison official today when he called him, asking that he consider donating a kidney to Joey in order to save his life. "Why should I?" he had cried into the phone. "My brother's nothing to me. And he's no good anyway."

"Actually he is," came the reply. "He's found God and works with the chaplain. Leads Bible studies and ministers to the inmates here. He has become a wonderful man who will benefit society when he's paroled. That is, if he gets a new kidney so that he can live long enough to get out."

Adam simply hung up. He was not going to lose the life he worked so hard to create to help a brother he didn't any longer know or want to know. His own family didn't even know about him and he would keep it that way. After all he'd done to be successful and get his fine family, he was not going to risk losing them.

He sniffed. What if he was too busy to spend a lot of time with them? He knew they thought he neglected them. He didn't mean to. But he had choices to make about how he would spend his every minute. And he always chose to concentrate on making money so they could have the best of everything. And besides, Marilyn no longer seemed to miss him.

He snorted dismissively. All his wife seemed to do was enjoy spending his money on homes, charities, that snooty church and the children he hardly knew who he thought of as university graduates without an ounce of ambition. His daughter Vicki spent all her time partying. And Bobby only wanted to build homes and training centers for the homeless.

As he remembered last night's conversation with his son, Adam shook his head as though trying to clear cobwebs from his aching brain. Bobby, with Marilyn's delicate features and the bright, gray eyes he vaguely recognized were the same as his father's, had timidly entered his study. "Dad," he said, "I have finally decided what I want to do with the rest of my life. And it's going to knock your socks off!"

Adam braced himself from behind his desk and raised a curious eyebrow.

"I want to help people who need help and are homeless. I want to give them places to live and job training so that they can get back on their feet." He shook his youthful head and his hair, the identical shade of his own, flopped over his forehead. "The government says they have programs to help but they don't do much. And there's such a long waiting list. People get lost in the crowd. We can create a foundation to help people sooner. And it'll be more effective." He held out a thick file. "I've put everything down on paper for you to study. I think you'll find that I've thought of everything. And if I haven't," he grinned, "I know you will. But there is one thing we have to move fast on. There's this old Victorian house near downtown. It's for sale and I heard that a glue company is thinking of buying it to turn into a factory. It would make a much better training center. So I'd like for you to go with me to see it right after Christmas. That is," suddenly his youthful face grew sober, even somewhat fearful," if you like my idea."

Adam had taken the file and promised his son that he would study it. But in his heart he knew there was no way that he would give his hard earned money to a bunch of bums even if it was his son's passion.

Realizing the little chapel was filling; he scrutinized the people who had sought refuge from the weather. Most of them looked decent enough. But there was a man who looked like someone his Bobby, with youthful naivety, wanted to save. Types like his birth family. People he'd spent his life trying to forget.

His gaze fell once again upon the window depicting Christ hanging on the cross between the two criminals. *What kind of man would give his life for bums like that?*

Suddenly clear words entered his very being. "Someone who knew that to gain his life, you have to lose it."

Adam's body jerked and his heart fluttered as he looked around him.

The voice continued. "My son, you have been so busy fleeing from the past that you have never really lived. You have gained the world but lost your soul!"

Adam started to shake and his stomach clenched fearfully. *Who knows the truth about me?* Tears started flowing down his face as he frantically swiped at them with the back of his trembling hand. He never cried. Not since that long ago time when they took Joey to Juvenile Hall and he had become totally alone. His legs quivered and he desperately wanted to run away. But his body felt too heavy to move. It was as though an unseen force was holding him down.

"You are finally facing the truth about yourself," the voice said. "And it scares you because now you're going to have to do something about it."

Adam's jaw tightened. This crazy thing—this mysterious voice—couldn't be happening! He was just imagining things because he was so tired and frustrated. He looked frantically around him. Who could possibly have said that to him?

"None of these people spoke to you. They can't even hear what you hear."

Then who...

"God. I spoke to you."

A terror covered Adam, giving him chills that turned his whole body into a quivering mass. It was the same feeling that had upset him whenever he was going to a new foster home. *God? Wh—why have you come to me?*

"Because I've finally got your attention. You can't run away from me here."

What—what do you want?

"I want you to change your ways. You need to. Badly!"

Without conscious thought, he turned his head to once again study the thief beside Christ. He reminded him of Joey.

"You must help your brother. That's one of the first things you must do."

Stiffening, Adam scoffed as he regained a tiny bit of his normal composure. He didn't care what this God thought. Joey wasn't worth it. After all, he was nothing but a lousy thief.

"You know he's not the only thief in your family."

Adam sat up straighter. *Wh - what do you mean?*

"You know very well what I mean. You stole Markowitz's

candy recipe for your own gain. And it has always bothered you. Even though you've tried not to think about it. Why, you're every bit as much a thief as your brother is. You just don't want to admit it."

Adam slumped in his seat and stared at his wet shoes. Shame cast a dark shadow over him as he nodded his head. Suddenly nausea grabbed his insides and he covered his mouth, willing himself not to be sick.

"So yes," the voice continued. "You certainly should help Joey. Besides you'll be benefiting more from doing that than he will."

I don't understand. Adam's thoughts spoke as clearly as though he spoke them out loud.

"You will in time."

Adam took a deep breath, trying to regain his characteristic control. It was the craziest thing he had ever done—to mentally talk to a faceless voice that claimed to be God. Yet strange as it seemed, he wanted to continue this silent conversation.

Wh—what else do you want from me?

"I want you to make amends with Markowitz and his sister. You stole from them. Now you must pay them back."

They're still alive?

"Barely. He's in a convalescent home. She's trying to stay in the house she raised you in. But she can't take care of it anymore. And there's very little money to help her." The voice, while firm, was surprisingly gentle. "They lost a lot when your candy bar beat theirs and became number one in sales."

Adam gulped. *I don't know how I can face them. I'm so ashamed.*

"You can swallow your considerable pride and just do it. And I'll be with you."

They'll think I'm awful. Which I am. They probably won't even want to see me.

21

"Yes they will. They think of you often. Always with love. They will forgive you."

Adam sat very stiff and silent while his heart hammered and his brain churned. Next thing this voice would probably want was for him to give Bobby that silly foundation.

"Yes. I want you to give your wonderful son his foundation. And I want you to cut back on your work to help him with it."

Adam started to shake violently again. Of all the requests, that was the craziest. Surely if this voice was really God's, he would know that he couldn't afford to cut back on his work. Especially if he was to financially help the Markowitzes. Besides didn't God know all about the money Marilyn gave to charities for him?

"You can do a lot more than donate that little bit that benefits your taxes. And certainly you can afford to cut back on your work that you only do to avoid really living and loving people."

The shivers rolling up Adam's spine felt like tiny bugs as he considered how well the voice knew him. Maybe this really was God. He shook his head as he thought about giving up the safety net that was his beloved work. He couldn't do it. He just couldn't.

"Yes you can."

Adam clasped his hands together and stared at the floor. If he were to quit working what would he do for money?

"You already have more than enough."

Adam's lips formed words he did not speak out loud. But he knew that somehow the voice—this God—could hear him think. "But without my work what would I do?"

"For starters, you can live honestly. Stop the lies. And you can reach out to others. People who need a helping hand. Poor little kids like you once were. There's a lot that you can do. Which is something your son seems to well understand."

Adam sighed and his mouth lifted into half a smile. *Well,*

maybe I could buy Bobby that house he wants. At least I can look at it with him.

"Good! You can see it tonight when the storm stops. It's right across the street."

As suddenly as it had come, the voice faded as the organ started to play "Joy To The World". A strange yet wonderful peace started pulling out all the heavy, bitter frustration from Adam. Amazed, his heart soared as all the unbearable weights he had carried all his life suddenly evaporated from him. For the first time he felt truly free and happy as tears rolled down his cheeks. Now he didn't care if anyone saw them. Embarrassment, for the first time in his memory, seemed to no longer matter.

While still crying, he laughed too as he offered a small salute to Christ on the cross. He felt like a modern Scrooge given a new lease on life.

He looked at his feet sliding on the maroon carpet and realized that what before appeared worn now looked like velvet. He leaned comfortably back in the pew and felt his mouth widen into what he knew was a giant, even silly, grin. Adam rubbed his hand over it. He couldn't remember ever grinning so broadly. Not in his entire lifetime.

He could hardly wait for the storm to end so he could get home to his family. And especially to Marilyn. To tell her of what he had learned in this little chapel and what he wanted to do with the rest of his life. And about Joey and who he really was.

For a second, a tiny frown dented his brow. Quickly, he wiped it away. *Surely, my wife will love the new me. Won't she?*

CHAPTER 3

$\cdotp\!\!\blacklozenge\!\!\cdotp$

The Heartbroken Widow

Elizabeth Curtis hugged her tote bag close to her breast as she stopped in front of the little chapel. She looked up at the blue illuminated cross that shone from its steeple. It beamed a warm welcome as snowflakes swirled around her with ferocious intensity while people jostled her as they trudged toward the church's door. Their footsteps were slow and heavy, making them look as though they were walking through quicksand.

Cold and wet, she joined them. While she did want to die, she certainly didn't want to do it by freezing. As she climbed up the chapel's snow covered steps, she glanced back down the street toward her bank that she had just left. Its sturdy brick building was almost lost in the white curtain of snow.

"What a fool I was," she scolded herself as she stepped through the door, held open for her by a pretty young girl with sad eyes. She gave her a curt nod then moved into the sanctuary. Walking slowly down the center aisle, she chose a seat in the right cluster of pews, close to the stained glass pictures of the young Jesus.

Now that she finally decided what to do about her tragic situation, she considered herself already emotionally dead. And by midnight tonight she would be completely dead. Put out of all her terrible misery and the awful emptiness.

With eyes still closed, she reached inside her bag. Her fingers flitted over its many contents—a wallet, checkbook, cosmetic bag, vial of pills, lots of tissue and her keys. These were not the items she was seeking. Her fingers continued digging and prodding until they found their target, a thick envelope that had settled on the bottom. Her hand squeezed it as she sighed. If her son Jim had been on her account she wouldn't have had to come out in this dreadful weather. But she never thought about putting him on it after Big Jim died. Just as she'd never had to concern herself with any money matters because her husband always handled that like he did everything important in their lives.

Tears rolled slowly down her cheeks and she felt their wet tracks glide over her gently lined face. Up until a year ago, when she was only seventy-five, people had judged her to be at least ten years younger. And she knew that they were right because her life had been pretty much stress-free. Any problems they had were quickly and efficiently taken care of by her Big Jim.

"He was so smart and wise. My wonderful Big Jim," she told herself as she reached inside her tote for a tissue. She smiled as she always did whenever she said or thought of her husband's nickname. His official name, which he explained with mock pompousness, was James Albert.

"But anyone who knows me for five seconds knows I'm more a Jim," he always boasted. That's what he had told her when she met him.

It had been a rainy day in May when she left her warm office with neither an umbrella nor a raincoat. She was rushing to renew her automobile insurance because, not having noted when it was due, she hadn't paid it. Now she'd just received a terrifying letter from her insurance company. By 12:01 in the morning, it warned, her insurance would lapse.

Desperate to avoid that, she hurried out in the rain and drove to the agency where, a year earlier, she purchased the insurance. Then she had been fresh out of high school and her Ford sedan, which was a masterpiece to her even if it was "previously owned", was her first car.

Soaked to the skin, she knew she was a wet mess as she stepped into the office and looked for the older man who helped her before. Instead she found a young man. His smile stretched across his face and made his blue eyes bounce.

"Hi Pretty Lady!" he said as he came up to her. "What can I do to help you?" His voice, full of energy, was a match for his jovial face.

"I—ah—I'm looking for Mr. Swift."

The man, who appeared to be just a bit older than her, towered above her. Taking her elbow, he led her to a small office. "Lenny is recovering from surgery. I work for him."

He waved her to the chair in front of a desk scattered with piles of papers. "I'm sure I can help you," he said as he reached out his hand.

She obediently responded. Smiling, he took her hand in both of his and held it in such a warm grasp that it felt like a caress. "I'm James Albert Curtis," he explained. "But anyone who knows me for more than five seconds—and that includes you because you've been here for at least one minute—knows I'm more of a Jim."

He laughed and she noticed that it seemed to bubble up from deep within him. "Don't you think that's right?" he asked.

She stared at him, unsure of what he meant. "Right? About what?"

He gave her that big grin again. "About me being more a Jim than a stuffy old James Albert?"

"I—I guess so." She removed her hand from his grasp and

squeezed the handle of her purse as the rainwater on her hair dripped onto her face.

He flopped into his chair, grabbed a tablet from underneath one of his stacks of papers and leaned forward. His face, that moments before was so happy, became serious. As she looked at him, she couldn't decide which look made him more attractive—the happy or the serious.

"You look like a lady who has a problem." His tone was laced with concern. "Maybe a big one?"

She nodded and started to open her mouth to speak.

He held up his hand. "Before you tell me what it is, I can promise you that no matter what it is, I can fix it. So tell me all about it." He grinned again, causing her to decide that the happy face won as her favorite. She took the lapse letter from her purse and handed it to him. "I—I forgot to pay this. I—I'm so dumb when it comes to money."

"No you're not! You just have more important things to do. Like being beautiful."

She blushed as he took the letter from her hand. While she was petite with a decent figure and a face that her parents and friends told her was attractive, she had never considered herself even remotely beautiful. Or even pretty. And she was so shy that few boys had ever tried to talk to her long enough to take her seriously. The few dates she'd had in high school had been one time events. She hadn't really minded. An only child born to people already middle aged, she was more comfortable with adults than kids her own age. What she enjoyed most was doing things with her parents who had petted and spoiled her with ecstatic adoration. Now that she was out of school, she had foregone college to work for her accountant father as his secretary.

Looking at Jim's messy desk, she couldn't help but compare it to her father's meticulous one.

He read the letter in mere seconds. "Don't worry about this. I'll get you an extension if you need one."

"No. No I don't. I have the money." She reached into her purse and pulled out her checkbook. Flowers and purple butterflies decorated its cover.

He grinned. "You like flowers. And butterflies."

She squirmed. "Yes I do."

"I knew you would. Even before I saw that."

"Can I pay you? How do I do this?" Her pen was poised over her checkbook.

"Let's make this really easy for you." He punched numbers into a calculator, then looked up and smiled. "Just write the check—made out to Crown Auto Insurance—for twenty dollars. Then we'll set you up so that the company can automatically take twenty out every month from your checking account. That way you never have to worry about writing another check or forgetting to pay and losing your insurance." He smiled again. "How does that sound?"

"Wonderful!" She quickly wrote the check and handed it to him. "How can I thank you? I was so worried."

"That's easy! After we fill out the bank draft form, you can go to dinner with me." He glanced at his watch. "It's almost five. Dinner time."

She looked down at her feet and felt her face grow hot. She was sure she was blushing. "Oh I—I don't know," she finally stammered. "I'm not usually very good company."

His eyes, the color of cornflowers, twinkled. "You let me be the judge of that Miss Elizabeth Newton."

That dinner changed her life. By the end of the evening she had fallen madly in love with him. And miracle of miracles, it seemed he felt the same about her. She couldn't believe that someone as dashing, handsome and charming as Jim could want her. It both thrilled and terrified her. After all, what would she do if he ever decided she wasn't good enough for him? But his ardor for her never waned as he spent every minute he could spare, when he wasn't selling insurance, with her. Five months later they became engaged.

He had dazzled her mother from the beginning. "He's such a nice young man," Ida said. "So good looking and outgoing. I like him."

Her overly protective and most cynical father had a different opinion. "He's alright I guess. But," Wesley Newton shook his head. "I don't like his commission only job. Doesn't offer much security. I'd rather you fall for someone with a regular paycheck. Someone with a good, steady corporate job."

When Jim respectfully asked him for permission to marry Liz, as he called her, he surprised his future father-in-law by whipping out his commission statements for the last three years. They were five times larger than her father made from his thirty-year-old business.

"I guess Jim will be able to take good care of my little girl after all," he said as she and her mother enthusiastically planned an elaborate wedding to be held one year later, on the date when the young couple met.

When she walked down the aisle in her white satin wedding gown, it was the only time that Elizabeth was a star. After that, and for the rest of their life together, she had continued to be so madly in love with him that she happily, lovingly and most willingly lived in her Jim's shadow.

Or, as he had become on the day of their son's birth, her Big Jim. He had insisted on giving the baby his name. "Then maybe if he has a son someday he'll give him my name too. Then there'll always be a James Albert." His grin, always so bright and youthful even as he grew older, convinced her.

"But what will we call him?" she asked. "Jim Two? Junior?"

"Lord no! I don't like juniors! How about Jim? Like me?"

She laughed as he kissed her hand. Their baby was only two hours old and she figured, with all the vanity of her twenty years, that she must look a fright from her long labor and delivery. But when her young husband entered her room after seeing his son through the nursery window, he pronounced both mother and son beautiful.

Now they were faced with naming their child—something they had refused to do before the birth. "When we see the baby we will come up with a name," they explained to concerned friends, family and particularly her father, who wanted everything handled with orderly preparation.

Now they had selected the obvious name for their son. Yet Jim's idea had caused Elizabeth some concern.

"How will you know who I want?" she asked. "If I call Jim you'll both answer me."

"How about Little Jim? For the baby of course."

Eyeing his six foot four, two hundred pound frame, she giggled. "With you for a father I doubt if he'll ever be little." She pressed his hand to the side of her cheek. "He already weighs eight and a half pounds you know. And is twenty inches long." Her eyes, which he described as a deep blue bordering on violet, caressed him.

He grinned. "Okay Liz. Then how about renaming me?" He stuck out his chest and pounded it like a gorilla, causing her to laugh again. "How does Big Jim sound?"

She held out her arms as he moved into them. "Wonderful! And most appropriate!"

And so he had become Big Jim and the baby just Jim. It was strange, she often thought, that they never called their son Jimmy—even when he was little. Her husband's edict was that they would always be Big Jim and Jim.

They had been such a happy family. When Jim was two they decided to have another baby. But ovarian cysts, which had to be removed along with her ovaries, kept that from happening. She had been devastated that there would be no more children. But her husband wasn't. "Honey! Our Jim more than makes up for a bunch of kids. With just him, we can really be the Three Musketeers."

And that's what they had been, going on long vacations as well as short day trips together. Outgoing like his father, Jim played every sport and they were at every game, cheering him on in their own ways. She sat quietly, squeezing her purse and praying, then smiling shyly whenever Jim made a touch down, shot a basket or hit the ball. Big Jim, of course, cheered louder and longer than anyone, his bombastic voice resembling the noisiest foghorn. *Then he'd lose his voice. And I'd have to feed him hot orange juice with honey to soothe his sore throat.*

She laughed. *How alike my Jims were. And how they loved being together.*

Then their two became three when Jim had his son, also officially named James Albert but called Jimmy. Big Jim, Jim and Jimmy. They had been so close and so happy. Then, in a split second, everything had ended.

Her tears flowed faster and she pulled another tissue out of her tote. She hugged the bag tightly against her, willing it to give her comfort. She couldn't believe she had any tears left after all the crying she'd done. And today marked the one year anniversary of the day when her life officially ended. On that fateful December 23, a year ago, Big Jim was on his way home from the agency he had bought from his employer and Jim had joined after college. He was as familiar with the highway he was driving on as he was of the street in his own neighborhood.

It had been a beautiful late afternoon with no snow or even rain. Not like the weather New Stockford was suffering with this year. One minute he was listening to his favorite tape of Elvis. Then suddenly he suffered a massive heart attack that led to a car crash. "Thank God no one else was hurt," she reminded herself for the millionth time, recalling that his sedan, in his favorite color of red, had smashed into the cement divider of the highway at eighty miles an hour. He hadn't worn his seat belt so his body was mangled, making survival impossible had the heart attack not killed him.

She glared at the large cross by the altar. She had always believed devoutly in the kind Heavenly Father preached about from the pulpit of her Lutheran Church. Then Big Jim died. "Where had God been," she had cried. Why couldn't He have given them a warning that her husband had a bad heart? Why couldn't God have made him sick so the doctor could find his heart condition and fix it? They were all questions she had asked with body jerking sobs thousands of times during the past year. And she never got an answer.

Her jaw hardened. *Did you try God? I know—I know. He cancelled his last two physicals. Said he felt fine and was too busy to bother with such time wasting nonsense.*

She fingered her hair, which she had allowed to go naturally white after years of dying it a soft brown to please him. This year, this empty year as she thought of it, she had allowed herself to age because there was no reason now to keep herself up.

She pushed a wisp of it from her face. *I should've gotten tough with him. Insisted that he keep those appointments* But she had never been able to get tough with him. Nobody could. Not even Jim who had more influence with his father than anyone.

Her son tried to console her when she expressed those regrets. "Dad was stubborn, Mom. You know that better than anyone. And if you had fussed at him—well," Jim shrugged, "Dad would've been more determined than ever not to see Doc Menske."

She knew her son was right. Just as she knew others were right when they consoled her with that oft-repeated cliché—"at least Big Jim went fast, with no terrible illness to suffer through." How she had grown to hate that statement even if it was true. Her heart actually moaned as she longed to scream at the well-wishers. "What about me?" she secretly cried. His sudden death wasn't good for me. I had no chance to prepare for a life without him. No chance to even consider such a thing."

Her chin trembled as she stared at the pulpit. Big Jim had been her world. They had fifty-five years together—a lifetime of love and togetherness. And it had ended so abruptly. She knew now that she could no longer go on living. It was a fact that she finally mustered the courage to face.

Although in the beginning, she had tried to keep going. Jim, of course, continued to run the insurance business, which had been named Curtis and Son Insurance when he had joined his father. He had even insisted on paying her what had been his father's share of the monthly income.

"I don't want it. Don't need it," she told him. "You have to do all the work now. You should have all the money."

"That's okay Mom. I can afford it." He smiled and her heart heaved as her husband's exact big grin shone from the face of her son. "Besides most of the accounts were Dad's before I joined him."

She knew that wasn't entirely true. That their son brought in most of the new business in the last few years had been a source of great pride to Big Jim. But she didn't argue because she knew that it would do no more good with Jim than it had ever done with his father. So she accepted the monthly checks and tried to build a life as a widow.

Widow! How she hated that word! It suggested uselessness, old age, sexlessness, stupidity and dependence. It was the title of irrelevant people with nothing more to live for.

Her friends, many widows or divorcees themselves, invited her to women only dinners, bridge clubs, Bunko parties and charity fashion shows where the featured clothes were too youthful and small for any of them. Her church, which she had enthusiastically served with her husband by her side, asked her to lead women's groups and Bible Studies. But she wouldn't do anything for God after what He had done to her.

Finally she just gave up trying to cope with her empty life. She no longer went out with friends or even answered their calls. Nor did she go to her quilting classes or even make any quilts, which used to be her greatest passion after being her husband's wife.

She even tried to stop seeing Jim and the kids. She twisted her gloved fingers and huddled forlornly in her pew. She hadn't been able to avoid Thanksgiving just a few weeks ago and it had been awful. Throughout the day, she remembered that bittersweet time last year when her husband had been with them, jovially carving the turkey and teasing the children about who they thought could eat the most—their daddy or their grandpa.

Of course he won. He always did. She laughed. *That man sure did love to eat.*

Then three weeks later he had died and taken with him her very life. Now her world had become a dark gray and not even her beautiful grandchildren could add any joyful color to it.

"I know today was hard for you," her son said as he drove her home after the big holiday dinner. "But it will get better with time. You must believe that."

She simply muttered and hurried out of his car as soon as he stopped in front of her house. That's when she made up her mind. When she walked into that big empty house and realized it would always be empty and she would always be alone. Right then and there, she decided to put an end to her miserable existence. She justified her intention by telling herself that she was doing it for Jim too because she knew that the way she was—so miserable and pathetic—was a terrible burden to her beloved son and his family.

Methodically, with a calmness that surprised her, she started plotting exactly what she would do. Having taken sleeping pills ever since Big Jim's death, she had just refilled a ninety-day supply the day before Thanksgiving. But not sure those ninety pills would be enough to kill her; she called her doctor for a new prescription. She actually lied to their family doctor, Doc Menske, by telling him that her purse had been stolen and her pills had been in it. He never doubted her, probably because he had known and trusted her for years. So he simply handed over a new prescription with no questions asked. And she went to a pharmacist different from her regular one to get the pills filled.

As she sat in the pew remembering how carefully she'd arranged everything, she frowned. She hoped Jim wouldn't blame the doctor when he discovered how he helped her end her life. She would have to explain how she fooled Doc in her suicide letter that she still had to write when she could get out of this place and get home. She had planned on spending this whole day writing it. Then, for a reason she couldn't understand, she decided to call the bank to be sure that her son's name was on her savings account as she wanted to be certain that he could withdraw all her money when she was gone.

But stupid me. They said I hadn't put him on it.

So she ventured out in the snowstorm to get her money. It had been fifty thousand dollars and the bank people hadn't wanted to give it to her. She thought they were afraid some scam artist was robbing her—probably because she was an old lady. But she told them that she was going to give ten thousand dollars to her son and each member of his family for Christmas. So they finally let her have it.

She chuckled. What a liar she had become after a whole lifetime of never even telling one single fib. But in a way she was telling the truth. Jim would find the big bundle of cash she now had in her tote. She would put it and her note on the stand beside her bed where she would lay after taking the pills and she knew that he would share it with his family.

She dared not think of her son arriving at her house tomorrow. He would be there to pick her up and take her to his home. There, she was expected to spend the night in order to enjoy all the early morning Christmas festivities with her grandchildren.

"Little Beth still believes in Santa," he reminded her just this morning as he laughed into the phone. "So you'll want to see her face when she sees all that Barbie loot old Santa's gonna haul down the chimney. And Sylvia is planning a wonderful dinner."

But what he'll find is my dead body. Guilt momentarily squeezed her heart and she shivered, willing it away. She knew that what she was doing was selfish and unloving. That it was probably the worse thing she could ever do to her family who would be heartbroken. To some people, committing suicide would be considered an awful sin. She knew that the church felt that way. But she couldn't help it. The pain of her loneliness and loss was just too severe for her to endure. She hoped they'd understand and forgive her. Especially when she explained that she couldn't help it. That much as she loved them she just loved Big Jim more.

"That's not true!"

She jumped as the angry words pummeled her brain.

"If you love Big Jim as much as you say you do—think you do—you would not do this."

Her breath caught, squeezing her chest as she looked around at the people sitting near her. *Who said that?* None of the people in the chapel paid her any attention. *Who said that?* Her mind screamed the question.

"Who do you think?"

She put her hand to her heart and frowned. It couldn't be Big Jim. And no one around her spoke. So could it possibly be..... *God?* She shook her head. Her depression was making her delirious. God couldn't possibly be talking to her.

"Oh but I am."

Heat started to flush her face and her back straightened. "If that's really you God go away," she screamed silently. "It's too late for you to come to me now. After you took Big Jim so suddenly! When you knew how lost I'd be without him!"

"I did know his death would hurt you Elizabeth. But I had to save him from a life of pain. And eventual paralysis that would have ended up being hell for both of you."

Every nerve in her body trembled as she strained to keep from crying out loud and ruining the silence of the chapel.

"He had Lou Gehrig's disease. Had it for years. Which would have been discovered had he gone for those physicals. He'd have eventually ended up unable to move. Yet knowing all too well what was happening to him."

She buried her face in her hands. *This can't really be happening. I must be insane.*

"No you're not."

She jerked her head and looked hastily around her. That voice was gentle, almost like her husband's. But it was impossible. Big Jim was dead. And yet...*Is that you Big Jim?*

"No Elizabeth. It's God. Big Jim is with me now. In heaven."

He's really with you? In spite of herself, she smiled.

"Yes he is."

Her chin trembled. *How is he?*

"He's fine. Very happy. Although he misses you. And is very upset that you want to end your life."

I can't help it! I miss him so much. Anger pulled her up stiffly. *Why did you have to take him from me? I would've taken care of him if he was ill.*

"My Dear Child, when you get up here you'll understand a lot of things. But until then, Big Jim and I want you to start living again. Embracing life again. As he always did. And as I created you to do."

I can't.

"You can. You must. For Big Jim. You are all that's left of him for your son and grandchildren. Jimmy and Beth need you."

Elizabeth knew better. Those children had their parents and didn't need her.

"But they do also need grandparents. And you're all they have. Love them for Big Jim. Hug them for him. Support and encourage them. This I ask you to do. If you really love Big Jim. And Me."

Elizabeth's stomach churned and she felt dizzy as she grabbed the back of the pew before her. She had always secretly wondered about life after death. Now that she knew Big Jim really was with God as her church had said, she felt a happy glow spring up within her. More than ever, she wanted to join her husband in heaven.

"It's not time for you to join your husband in Heaven," the voice said softly. "There's still much for you to do here. As you will see, your son especially will need you."

As she pondered those amazing words, she felt God's presence disappear like a floating cloud. She reached out her hand, trying to stop a being that her worldly eyes could not see but who her soul knew. She slowed her racing heart. She still had so many questions but she sensed that some day she'd find the answers. Meanwhile she had to figure out how to get back to living. She looked at the stained glass windows near her.

The first one was the nativity scene of Mary, Joseph and the baby.

Sweet young couple. Like Big Jim and I were when our son was born.

She turned her gaze to the second one and smiled faintly. Mary and Joseph were confronting the teen aged Jesus at the temple where he had been for several days; causing them great worry as they hunted for him. She and her husband had worries about their boy too. And on several occasions they also had to look for him.

Then she turned to look at the stained glass window on the other side of the room showing Mary standing at the foot of her son's cross. When they had killed Mary's son she had been alone. Without her husband just as Elizabeth was without hers. Her heart ached as she loosened her grip on her tote bag. Look what Mary had to endure. Did she ever consider ending her life when her loved ones died.

Suddenly the first dawning of hope warmed her heart. Her world, which had been so dark, started to fill with light.

Mary had other people who loved her just as she did. Elizabeth's white head nodded slightly. Now she understood that she was not the only woman who had lost a loved one and been heartbroken.

She felt God's presence return to her and her lips curved into the first joyous smile of the year. She would try to do what God would ask her to do. And she'd start by living again. Yet she still wasn't sure how to do that. She looked at the altar and her heart shivered at the sight of the tall cross. "Please be with me God," she whispered. "Help me! I can't—I just can't do it alone." A large lump started to lodge in her throat and she swallowed hard to push it down. "And also God, please, help me get over this terrible loneliness for my Big Jim."

CHAPTER 4

◆ ◆ ◆

The Lost Pastor

William Worth—known to thousands as Pastor Will—leaned against the back wall of the chapel and took in the entire room. It seemed cozy in an old, simple way that was a startling contrast to the metal and marble church he served. A corner of his mouth lifted. *How quaint.*

Still shivering from the bone biting cold that drove him into the small structure, he pulled the collar of his overcoat around his chin and over his ears and ducked into a back pew. Because he was tired, cold and not wanting to talk to anyone, he hoped that nobody would recognize him. But of course they wouldn't. He wasn't from around there. But if the new producers had their way, he guessed that everyone would soon know him.

He cringed as the small voice inside his soul posed the question that had been clawing at him for weeks. "Is that really what you want?"

Ignoring it, he settled into the wooden seat and allowed his body to relax as he slowed his breathing -- a technique he used to ward off anxiety that had become a part of him. The organ's programmed music was playing "Silent Night" and he felt its calming melody wrap around him like a cozy blanket. He closed his eyes. How restful and sweet this place was. It reminded him of the first church he had ever known, Christ Chapel.

His mind, usually so crowded with demands and deadlines, flashed upon a scene from long ago. It was of a small wooden church next to a quiet lake that had belonged to a Christian camp. Sponsored by an Interdenominational church, it had provided summer outreaches for inner city kids. He smiled wistfully. He had just been thirteen and it was his first Christian Camp and church. His family hadn't been at all religious. In fact, until his best friend, Artie Grant, witnessed to him, he'd never even heard of Jesus Christ.

In spite of those nativity scenes I thought Christmas was just about Santa Claus. And there had been very little from Santa Claus. Will's family was large and it took his father's two jobs and his mother's one to keep their six children outfitted in thrift store clothes, minimally fed and secure in one of many rundown houses they rented in even more rundown neighborhoods.

"You kids should be glad you have a roof over your head," his mother was fond of saying as they would climb into their old car, with bald tires, to drive to one of many soup kitchens.

So when Artie invited him to go with him to Christ Camp for a week on a scholarship, he had jumped at the chance. It would give him one blessed week free of the responsibilities of being the oldest child who was always taking care of younger siblings. And surprisingly, as long as it didn't cost them anything, his parents let him go.

That camp changed his life. He'd been shorter than most of the boys his age and spoke with a stutter that prompted embarrassing imitation from his schoolmates. "H- h- h- here c -c- c- comes l- l- l- little W- W- Will," they'd tease whenever they say him.

But at the camp those same kids, as well as others, were

discouraged from ridiculing anyone. And there were lots of kids with worse problems than his. Kids in wheelchairs; with cleft palates; those who were blind or mentally retarded. But at camp everyone had value and was loved. There had been absolutely no cruelty of any kind at that wonderful place.

He looked at the stained glass window portraying Jesus. Christ's love was so real and alive there. It had been incredibly wonderful. That love was what made him walk down the center aisle of Christ Chapel when the Youth Minister, who was barely eighteen years old, invited them to give their lives to Jesus. To accept His death so that Will, and all sinners, would not die but have eternal life.

"For God so loved the world that He gave His only begotten son," Will reminded himself. "That whosoever believes in Him will not perish but have life everlasting." He rubbed his fingers across his forehead and the lines that etched his brow seemed to mock him. *So much has happened since I so innocently and seriously believed that statement. And made it the foundation of my life.*

He stared at the empty cross behind the altar and bit his tongue to hold back the great urge to scream. He had moved so far from God and what he once was. And now he was considering a future that would make him even more famous! Which he knew in his heart of hearts he really didn't want. So what was he thinking to go ahead with this plan?

As if looking for a rare jewel, he allowed his mind to search back through time to those early, wonderfully innocent years. After his dedication to Christ, his life seemed charmed. Where before he was a defiant student, he settled down and started seriously studying. And every day he prayed—not that God would remove the curse of his stuttering but that He would enable him to learn to live with it. But God did cure it by taking it completely away.

And then God gave him the gift of a good singing and

speaking voice. And eventually, He even made him, if not tall, at least not small anymore. So he could hold his own with the other guys. While still in school he had joined a Christian Boys' Quartet—The Singing Saints—and for a while he thought music was what God wanted him to do with his life. Then, five years later at eighteen, he was a counselor at the same camp and gave his testimony to lost kids like he had been. And when he invited them to come forward to accept Christ, most of them responded to his impassioned plea. It was an experience that greatly impressed the adult camp leaders.

"You have a true gift," they told him, admiration shining from their eyes. "You must go into the ministry. Become a Minister."

And so he had, winning scholarships to college and seminary and then going on to get his Doctor of Divinity degree. And along the way, he led his family to Christ. He smiled at the thought of his five siblings and parents. Now they were all devout, active Christians who were raising fine families and serving in churches all over the country. Besides reaching family and friends, he stood on street corners playing his guitar, singing and loudly preaching to anyone who would listen that they needed to repent of their sins and turn to Jesus.

He grinned at the memory. How he had loved his life serving God with such zeal! Eventually, when he landed his first job with Pastor Kingman, he gave that up and became more conservative in the way he presented Christ. He frowned. Maybe that had been his first mistake and started his downfall. But he wouldn't have known that then.

His enthusiasm, winning personality and scholarship along with his fervent dedication to Christianity had won him the job as Youth Pastor at the four hundred-member church called Elm Street Community. Located on a street where tall, ancient elm trees stood like stalwart soldiers by the curb, it was an imposing building of red brick with a great white steeple. It was known for its family oriented teaching and activities; and he had been thrilled to work with the distinguished pastor who had started the church in a garage.

Pastor Todd Kingman was an imposing figure. He had the body of a big barrel and a bald head with a full, gray handlebar mustache. While his physical presence was impressive, his personality was down right intimidating. To Will he was the strongest, most self-assured person he had ever seen. While the church's constitution called for its governing to be done by a board of nine men, everyone knew that Elm Street Community was really Kingman's domain and he ruled it with a strong hand, iron will and defiant stubbornness that discouraged anyone from crossing him.

But Will didn't care about—let alone even recognize—the politics and intrigue that was whirling around him from the beginning. Instead he threw himself into his job of building up the youth program, which was the only ministry in the church that was lacking vibrancy. *I'll admit it. I was eager to build a name for myself. And also to impress Becky.*

He smiled as he recalled the first time he saw Pastor Kingman's daughter. Will had only been at the church three days when he saw her, standing between her father and mother, greeting people as they entered the sanctuary. Even then he knew that the pretty girl with the blonde ponytail was "Thee One". That realization was solidified at the end of the service, when she sang one of his favorite hymns, How Great Thou Art. His heart soared and he felt that no angel in all of Heaven could have done a better job.

Rebecca, "Becky", Kingman was the only child of Todd and Rachel Kingman and had been raised since babyhood to serve the church with the devotion of her parents. Consequently, she knew what a woman who belonged to a man of God was supposed to do—be supportive at all costs, never say anything that could be construed as controversial or judgmental, always give in to the wishes and needs of others, look just good enough to be considered attractive but play down any beauty that would make others jealous and make no demands on your husband, especially if they would keep him from serving his flock.

He looked up at the ceiling and smiled. It hadn't taken him long to win her. He'd always known that God had a hand in that. And Pastor Kingman too, who Will suspected had hired him as much to marry his daughter as for what he could do for his church. And God and his mentor had been right. He and Becky were perfect together, considered by many to be a regular Christian Barbie and Ken. They were married just six months after he joined the church.

By then he had tripled the attendance of the youth group and when the Assistant Pastor died suddenly of a heart attack, William took over his job with Kingman's blessing.

Everything had been perfect for a while. The twins, Danny and Dottie, came along a year later and the church grew.

Then the problems started. He frowned. He could exactly pinpoint when ill feelings between his father-in-law and him started. It was when he started preaching the sermon on the first Sunday of every month. The elders had pressed Kingman hard to let him do that. They argued that it would give the older man a rest and even a day off if he wanted one.

And it would give Will some preaching experience. Kingman had been forced to go along with it even though Will knew it wasn't what he wanted. But the young preacher didn't care. He was just eager to be up there in that pulpit, to talk about God and bring folks to Him. And, perhaps most of all, to show Becky's Dad that he could be like him. Maybe even better.

Very soon attendance was greatest on William's Sunday. Then he was being requested to officiate at weddings and even funerals—two events that Todd Kingman had always guarded as his own. Will knew that God had made that happen by giving him the words to say. And, he had to admit, the success had been so exciting and ego filling!

Then one day it all came to a head. Dad, as Kingman had

encouraged Will to call him, invited him into his office. When he got there, he was told to close the door and sit down. As soon as Will did, a piece of paper was thrown at him. It was a letter from an old friend, asking if Kingman or someone he knew would be interested in being the pastor of a new church one thousand miles away.

"It would be a great opportunity for you," his father-in-law said. "You could start your own church. Do your own thing. Not be held back by me or the board. And you know that can be difficult. Even stifling."

"But I like it here. I'm doing just fine. I think?"

"Yes you are doing well." Becky's father sighed heavily as he looked at him from behind his paper-cluttered desk. Suddenly he looked old, exhausted and even beaten. "Alright William, let me tell it like it is. I want you to leave. Because - because if you don't it will be just a matter of time before they throw me out in favor of you."

Will had waved away those words. "No Sir. That would never happen. It couldn't. This—this church is all yours. You built it. Why, you are Elm Street Community. Everybody knows that."

Todd shook his head as beads of perspiration glistened on his bare head that was such a sharp contrast to Will's thick, sandy hair. "I appreciate what you're saying," he said. "For the most part, it's true. I've sweat blood for this church. Even helped lay the foundation with my own hands. But I also know that if the board really wanted to get rid of me and there was someone available who was young, popular and able to replace me, they'd do it." He snapped his pudgy fingers. "They'd do it in a heart beat. Especially since I've upset all of them at least once with our many power struggles. So my boy," he forced a jovial strength to his voice, "I sense it's just a matter of time before the axe falls. And God help me I don't want to be replaced by anyone. Least of all a young, gifted man like you." He forced a wan smile. "Don't get me wrong Boy. I love you. I'm proud of you. But, well, you are just so much better than I ever thought you'd be." He leaned across his desk. "Don't you understand? I'm fighting for my life here. This church—it's my life."

"But what about Becky? She won't want to move."

"She'll go wherever you go. She's been trained to be a good wife."

In the end, he had landed the job and his wife had dutifully, though somewhat tearfully, followed him just as her father had promised. If she had misgivings about the move or felt anger, he was never aware of them. But then, he'd never asked her what she wanted to do. Nor, for that matter, about anything.

And it had been so exciting. They started with a little storefront church and built it into a big campus with a thousand seat auditorium and a school from kindergarten to twelfth grade. Most miraculous of all was that they did it all in just ten years

He looked down at his feet, clad in three-inch shoes to give him height, and sighed. He knew that it was God who built that church. And Will always gave Him the credit. But he also admitted, with a total lack of humility, that God had used him to get it done.

During those years, Will wrote books that led to hobnobbing with the rich and famous. Eventually he put his sermons on the radio—first one inexpensive station then to all the top ones in the region. And two years ago the television programs started, reaching audiences in four states. And that was probably when the trouble really started. Then again, he frequently wondered, it might have been sooner when he actually started compromising his beliefs and watering down his messages.

By the time he hit the television screens he knew that if he wanted to keep, let alone increase, both his audience and his donations that were so necessary to keep him on the air, he could no longer preach about sin and hell. In fact, he couldn't even really urge anyone to accept Christ. On the few occasions when he allowed himself to feel guilty about it, he told himself that in today's world he needed to preach the feel good stuff like positive thinking, politically correct acceptance and approval of everyone and everything. He'd willingly compromised all that he'd learned in seminary that was against what the Bible taught in order to keep his ministry alive. But he felt it was worth it because he reached people. And soon he'd be reaching even more.

Will's stomach twisted as he stared at the stained glass window of Christ praying in the Garden of Gethsemane. Why then did he feel like he was in his own Gethsemane? All his successes—the promise of real fame—really meant nothing to him now. He was just hollow inside and totally empty. He lifted his hands, and then allowed them to fall into his lap.

He tried to slow his breathing, but the breaths came in gasping speed. "You've given me so many blessings Lord," he prayed. "Wonderful people who helped me build my church." Hearing himself refer to the church he served as "my church" made him gasp with alarm. He sounded like old Kingman.

Deep furrows marked his face as he considered his father-in-law who had eventually lost his church to another preacher who replaced Will. Todd Kingman had been so angry that he sued the church and the elders. After a vicious and embarrassing court battle, he lost. It turned him into a bitter man who was angry at God. When he finally died from a stroke, Will, Becky and even his mother-in-law considered the old preacher's death a blessing.

Now Will was filled with terror as he compared himself to Todd Kingman. Surely he was not a dictator and egotist like he had been. He looked at his hands, shocked that they were trembling. *Oh God don't let me end up like Kingman. Please.*

He glanced at his watch and realized with a start that Becky would be expecting his plane to be landing in the airport of the town where they lived. It was five hundred miles from here in a pretty southern suburb where people didn't have to lock their doors. Where someone like him could become a celebrity. Had he called her that the planes weren't flying and he couldn't get home tonight?

He shrugged. He and his wife spoke so little to each other that it was highly unlikely he even thought to call her. Once, when they were first married, they had called each other all the time when parted. Now they were strangers who simply shared a house and a life for the sake of appearances. Yet Becky was still the obedient wife, standing by him every Sunday, sure that their charade convinced their people that they were happily married.

Actually they weren't really unhappy. They were just busy with other things, he convinced himself whenever he briefly dared to think about his marriage. Will tried to remember the last time they had gone on a real, non-church related, date. Or made love. Or, for that matter, even said "I love you" to each other.

He couldn't.

Christmas was in about thirty hours and he suddenly realized that he hadn't even bought Becky a gift yet. That was a first. Always before he'd at least taken the time to pick out something that she always pretended to like. But we did just get that new refrigerator, he thought. She probably assumes that's her Christmas present.

He cringed. That sounded awful and terribly indifferent. Which, if he was to be honest, was the problem. He was indifferent to his wife. On some level he probably still did love her because of the history they had together, but to love, desire and cherish her for her uniqueness like he used to? He shook his head. *No!*

In the peace of this chapel, he was forced to face the empty, melancholy life that was now his. And a great part of it was his indifference to Becky, who had always been so good, so helpful, so nurturing. Truly a pastor's dream wife who always served his flock with a smile while keeping his children from hurting his reputation.

Now the twins were twenty-five. Dottie, whose bout with

drugs had been well hidden when Becky sent her to a rehab center one thousand miles away, had straightened out and was now married and expecting her first child. Danny, who had always been a quiet, even shy kid, was a struggling artist in San Francisco. While he talked to them by phone at least once every other month and had promised to visit Dottie when her baby was born, Becky had remained much closer to their children. Visiting them at least four times a year, she had been wonderful about keeping him posted on how they were doing.

He really did need to make a point of seeing more of his kids. Especially now that they were older and he was about to be a grandfather. But then he also needed to make more time for Becky. Now that they no longer had kids at home, they should have grown closer. Taken trips and renewed their early courtship days. That was what people in their age group kept telling them to do. But he was always too busy.

He leaned over in the pew until his face was practically touching his lap, as though trying to hide but knowing he couldn't. *How could Becky and I have grown so far apart?*

"You know the answer to that!" The voice was deep and bold as it confronted his heart.

Startled, he straightened. *God? Is that you? Actually talking to me?* Warmth wrapped around him and he smiled. Yes that was God's voice. He did still know it—even though it had been a long time since he'd heard it. Or, for that matter, even listened for it.

"You decided to ignore your wife when you were courting the admiration of others. Especially the women. And the media and crowds. You allowed yourself to become a fancy peacock. And deep down, though you probably don't even realize it, you've always thought of your wife as a simple little peahen."

Will's mouth grew dry. It was true. He had considered Becky to be an accessory to him, like a lamp shade is to a lamp. Necessary but not the main attraction. Such a realization twisted his stomach, causing him to defend himself to the voice that was penetrating his soul. *I didn't mean to do that. It just happened. It wasn't my doing.*

"You allowed it. And you encouraged the women."

I needed a lot of help. And they gave it. But I've never touched any of them. You know that! He fidgeted as his mind faced another truth. Though he did have to admit that he'd been tempted.

"You've had emotional affairs by encouraging their confidences and accepting their help when Becky would have done it if you asked her. You know very well that many of those women are in love with you."

That's a problem all pastors have. Women are attracted to us because of the power of the pulpit.

"I know that. But with you, it's worse. You encourage them when most pastors know better."

Will slumped in his seat. *Yes God. I know. I'm sorry.*

"Then stop it. Go back to your first loves.....your love for me and your love for your wife."

What would you have me do? Even as he asked the question, Will feared the answer.

"Start by taking a really good look at your wife. She's still a beautiful woman who many men would love to have for a wife. Realize your good fortune and get to know her again. When's the last time the two of you had a conversation that wasn't about the church or your kids?"

Will shrugged. *I don't remember.*

"What's her favorite flower?"

I don't know.

"Her favorite color?"

Blue. I think.

"No. It's green. That's been her favorite since she decorated the children's playroom twenty years ago when they were five."

Will gulped. *I can't believe with all the big things happening in the world that God cares about a person's favorite color.*

"I most certainly do care about and know even the tiniest

details of all my children's lives. So you should definitely care about those of your wife."

Will sighed irritably. *O.K. I get it. I don't know my wife. I'll fix it.* Resentment at God's chastisement poked at him. What did the Bible say about that? Be grateful that your Father disciplines you because that means he loves you?

The voice sounded like it was chuckling. "It's true. But besides getting back with Becky, I want you to give up that ministry you really don't want and come back to me. Preach the messages people need to hear. Not what they want to hear but what they need to hear. Stop compromising and diluting My Words. Start serving people again."

I thought I was doing that. His answer sounded defensive to his own ears. He could imagine how it sounded to God.

"You used to be a good pastor. A real tribute to me. But you haven't been for a long time. What you are running now is a social gathering. With those potlucks, Saturday fun nights and positive thinking classes, you barely look at my book."

"I was trying to get them into church so they could learn about you," Will explained silently.

"Then why do you keep me on the shelf?"

I didn't know I was.

"You know you are! You no longer even invite anyone to come to me at the end of your sermons. Why is that?"

The elders don't want me to do that. They say it makes people uncomfortable. And—and sometimes when people won't come forward when I make the call I feel foolish. Embarrassed. I'm sorry. That's how I feel.

"William! William! William! Don't you know? It's never been about you! It's been about me. But you can correct it right now. Just do what I say—move back to the boy you once were. Remember him? On fire for me? You have so much more work to do. The plans I have for you will remove all that emptiness. Make you feel alive again."

Where will I go? What will I do?

"Look around you. This little church needs a pastor. This neighborhood needs revival. And the people here, they need your optimism and support."

For the briefest of seconds, his great church, television and radio ministries, books and hobnobbing with the rich and famous flitted across his consciousness. But he didn't consider them with regret. Rather Will was bidding them a grateful and eager farewell.

Then, just as he had when he first stepped into the little church, he again scanned the chapel. But this time Will studied it with a heart that saw possibilities. *This street, this church—I have to admit they remind me of my early days. Preaching on street corners.*

"You were happy then."

He grinned.

"You will be again."

Yes. Yes I will! Slowly, steadily, he stood and made his way to the front where he could better examine the Nativity Figures, the altar, the cross and the organ.

His smile stretched across his face. "I need to get a better look," he told himself. "Since I'll be spending the rest of my life here."

CHAPTER 5

The Reluctant Bride

Susie Porter wrapped the shawl collar of her faux fur coat around her neck and face and burrowed down in a corner of one of the chapel's pews. She shivered as a heavy chill invaded her bones. "But it's not from the weather," she told herself. "It's from the wedding. And what I know my life will be like when I marry Frank."

She stared at the woman sitting in front of her. In her mid fifties with bags surrounding her, she looked depressed and even beaten down. Like there was no joy in the season for her. That would be her after being married to Frank for a long time.

She shook her head. "No. That's me, most of the time, now. At least in my heart. So why are you going to marry him?" It was a question that she had asked herself constantly and now, with her wedding just seven days away, it was becoming a more frantic, even hysterical, challenge. And her answer was always the same. Because she had made a promise.

Their love affair, if it could be called that, had started in her senior year in high school. She had attended a party with her best friend Jennifer Riley. The memory of that event, which would turn out to be a great life changer for her, was as fresh now—five years later—as it was the day after it happened. She hadn't wanted to go. She was never one for parties but Jen insisted. Susie's lips drooped. Being the people pleaser that she was she had, of course, given in.

For a reason that she couldn't understand at the time, she put more than her usual careless effort into what she wore. This sudden interest in her appearance took her by surprise. Her older sister, Samantha, was the beauty in the family. Everybody admired her. Susie, on the other hand, was plain which made it necessary to work twice as hard to make the best of what little she had. Her biggest problem was her body. While Samantha and her mother were tall and willowy, Susie was short, with a tendency to carry an unneeded ten pounds around her hips, making her figure a challenge to dress. That night she had covered it with a new pair of jeans and a big shirt of blue and white stripes that promised a slenderizing effect. Silver heart earrings dangled from her ears. She had bought them especially to call attention to her round face and long hair. *I thought I looked really good that night. Even Mom complimented me.*

Yet when she and her friend arrived at the party, Susie immediately felt inferior to the crowd of kids who she knew were much more attractive than her. She had barely stepped inside before she was telling Jen that she wanted to leave. She laughed as she recalled her friend's response. "Oh Sus don't be such a nerd! We just got here. Chill and try to have fun."

First thing Susie did was what she always did when she was nervous. She headed for the food. "Which was the last thing I should've done." She was opening her mouth to bite into a chili covered hot dog when he spoke.

"Hi. I'm Frank Mercer. Who are you?"

With forced daintiness, she put the hotdog back on the paper plate and looked up to see a tall, well built young man with dark, wavy hair and the face of a Grecian God smiling down on her. "S- Susie. Susie Porter," she mumbled.

He flashed her a grin that turned her legs into jelly. "Hello Susie Porter. Glad to meet you." With one hand, he took her elbow and with the other her plate and guided her through the crowded room to a corner where two folding chairs sat unoccupied.

Obediently she sat on the one he led her to and primly took back her plate, although she knew she wouldn't eat a bite as there was nothing very attractive about gobbling on a chili dog. And she desperately wanted to look her best for him. As he sat beside her, their shoulders touched and her heart pounded.

I couldn't take my eyes off of him as we talked, she remembered. Now I don't remember what we even said. She shrugged. Actually Frank did most of the talking about himself. And Susie listened, absorbing the facts about his life as though she was a dry sponge slurping up water.

She couldn't believe that someone so gorgeous was interested in her and neither could Jen who looked at her with a shocked expression as she danced with a short guy with thick glasses.

That night Susie learned that Frank was already a junior at the university, majoring in business. He was an only child, son of a doctor, hated cats, and was a staunch Republican, a non-practicing Methodist and a jazz aficionado. "Don't bring a green vegetable near me," he laughed. "But I could eat up a whole corn field." He also lifted weights, worked out relentlessly every morning at five and most week-ends he ran in some kind of marathon.

His goal was to head his own corporation and be a millionaire by the time he was thirty. "I'll do it too. I've already designed my company. Software products that'll make Bill Gates drool."

As the party started to break up, he asked for her telephone number and promised to call. She gave it to him, with a voice she hoped didn't' sound too eager. But she never thought he would call as she assumed she was too dull and boring for someone as amazing as him.

The next morning, she was shocked when he called. "I'm taking you to a movie tonight," he announced. "Then dinner."

It hadn't occurred to her until she hung up that he hadn't asked if she was free or wanted to go. He simply ordered her to be ready—promptly at six he emphasized.

"And of course I was. Who wouldn't be for a guy like that?" she reminded herself. After the first date they saw each other as much as his schedule allowed.

Although bored with the whole affair, he had dutifully accompanied her to her senior prom. He had been so handsome in his black tux that all the girls envied her. She smiled at the warm memory. They couldn't believe that plain old Susie Porter could land such a hunk.

She loved every minute of their jealous looks. In fact she loved being seen with Frank. He had greatly raised her self esteem. Beside him, she felt important and like Somebody Special. She frowned. He also caused her to start acting like him—superior to everyone. It was an attitude she didn't like. Of course she also worked much harder at controlling her weight, dressing stylishly and enhancing, with the right make up and hairstyle, the good skin and cheek bones her mother said she had.

She needed to look at least somewhat like she deserved him. At least that was what her family said. "Frank is a great catch for any girl. That he seems to like you is nothing short of amazing luck," her mother had told her. "So whatever you do, don't lose him." What she didn't say but Susie knew she was thinking was that Samantha would have been a better choice for Frank.

And her sister, who could always get any man she wanted and yet was often dateless, simply wondered if Frank had a brother or cousin like him. Susie told her no. Which was the truth. The fact that she also didn't want Samantha pushing her way into that part of her life was the real reason. Because for once she had something better than her sister had and it felt wonderful. Especially after a lifetime of getting Samantha's hand me downs, rejects and being known as the nothing daughter.

But it wasn't only her outer appearance that Susie changed. She also changed who she was; becoming more the woman that Frank wanted her to be. She read all the books he told her to read and maintained friendships only with people he approved of. The opinions and thoughts she expressed were only those he had or approved of. She had become a good dutiful little puppet that would do or be anything to please her man.

And while she was losing herself, Frank was living his life exactly as he planned. He graduated from the university with honors and immediately landed a job with the most prestigious stock brokerage firm in the city. As he climbed up the executive ladder in record speed, he continued his plan to go into business for himself. So many times—more than she could even count—he consulted his computer planner and checked off his accomplishments with a proud smile. "Right on schedule," he would say.

Then he would turn to her. "How are you doing with your goals Susie?" he asked, even though he already knew the answer. It was his way of controlling her and he took heartless joy in doing it.

She went on to college—a state school that wasn't as prestigious as his university. *But it did the job. I graduated with honors too. Just like Frank. Although it didn't impress him.*

"You wouldn't have gotten such high grades if you'd gone to my university," he said. "So enjoy your little success."

She had. But her chosen profession, which she had selected to please him, left her cold. Instead of becoming a teacher, which had been her dream since kindergarten, Frank convinced her to major in business administration. "So you can work with me in my business," he explained. "That way it won't cost me as much money to get started. As my wife I won't have to pay you."

Since he hadn't started his business yet and didn't want her to work in anyone else's company, she took a part-time job in the children's section of the public library. And she loved it. Helping children find books for their school projects or for their reading pleasure didn't even seem like work. The thought of leaving the library to be employed by Frank filled her with a dread that made her hands sweat and her stomach cramp.

Her eyelids drooped as she petted her fur coat as though it was a cat—which she could no longer have because Frank hated them. She had given up herself for him. And now she didn't like who she'd become or what her life would become if she went ahead with that marriage.

Susie shivered as she remembered the scene at the courthouse today when they met to get their marriage license. The weather was terrible and she had begged him to wait until after Christmas when the weather report promised an end to the storm. But he wouldn't hear of it.

"You know very well that I'm going to Vegas with my friends on the twenty-sixth. I want you there today. Promptly at two."

Because the snow had slowed traffic she was ten minutes late. He was waiting, his face red with rage. "Honestly Susie! Can't you ever be on time?"

"I- I'm sorry. The weather. Traffic...."

He held up his hand to silence her. "Never mind your excuses. You're here now. "

He turned to the clerk. "Let's get this over with. I have to get back to the office."

The clerk was a small, gray haired man who reminded her of a gentle mouse. He had looked at her with so much pity, his face silently asking if she really wanted to marry such a rude man.

As the chapel's organ started to play Hark The Herald Angels Sing, she tilted her head to the side and put aside her earlier miseries. *That's what I need. A guardian angel to take me away from all this.*

Tears started to sneak into her eyes and she quickly blinked them away. She had already cried a million tears.

Her mother said it was just nerves. But Sarah Porter would say that. She loved the idea of her daughter marrying such a good looking, smart guy who was the son of a doctor. Frank was every mother's dream. Although Susie knew it was more her parent's dream for Samantha than for her as from the day she was born, her mother had been disappointed in her. And her father had wanted a boy.

Susie's parents never saw the controlling, rude side of Frank. To them he was perfect in every way. It was only when they were alone or with her friends, who he didn't like, that he showed his true colors. So how could she tell her folks that he was not what he seemed? That she wanted to cancel the wedding?

"I just can't," her mind whispered to her heart. "Not now that the wedding is already paid for. And the dress is hanging in my closet. The showers given. Gifts received. And all those people planning to come to my big, fancy wedding."

Then there were Frank's parents. They bought them their honeymoon cruise to Europe, booked the country club for the rehearsal dinner and made a big down payment on their house. At the thought of her future in-laws, tears did start rolling down her cheeks.

They were the best part of Frank. Thoughtful and kind, they were gentle people who were as unassuming as Frank was pretentious. His father was a cardiologist and she could imagine how safe everyone felt in his care. Frank's mother was short and plump with the sweetest smile Susie had ever seen. Mrs. Mercer loved to cook and bake and make guests in her home feel cherished.

Because they both seemed so different in personality to their only child, Susie wondered what made Frank so unlike them.

Then one day, when she was helping his mother wash dishes after an unusually big meal, Mrs. Mercer accidentally explained it. "When we adopted Frank," she said, "our life became complete."

"Frank's adopted?" Susie's expression, she knew, gave away her surprise.

Mrs. Mercer's hand fluttered to her mouth. "You didn't know? Oh Dear," she gasped. "It seems I've let the cat out of the bag." She gave Susie a reluctant smile. "I just assumed Frank would've told you."

Susie patted the older woman's shoulder and then gave her a hug. "I'm sure he intends to. And it really doesn't matter to me."

"Good!" Frank's mother sighed with relief. "So My Dear, why don't you just not say anything to Frank about you knowing. Wait for him to tell you. As I'm sure he will."

Susie nodded. "Of course. That will be best." Then, why she felt compelled to ask the question that she did, she didn't know. But for some reason—perhaps hoping to shine some light onto why Frank's personality was so different from his parents', she asked how old Frank had been when they adopted him. She had hoped they'd adopted him when he was a newborn so they could have totally formed his personality as Susie learned in psychology class that most people's personalities were formed by the time they were five. And if they experienced a lot of bad things, that could negatively affect them all of their lives.

Susie's heart seemed to fall through her feet when Mrs. Mercer told her he had been five when they got him out of the foster care system. When she timidly asked about his birth parents, her future mother-in-law's jaw tightened and her eyes suddenly avoided hers.

"We weren't told anything about them," she said quietly. "And we didn't care. All we saw was a lovely little boy." Then she looked back at Susie, almost glaring. "And look at him now! You couldn't find a more wonderful man. Why he's perfect. Isn't he Susie?"

"Yes," Susie whispered, though she only said that to please Mrs. Mercer.

But that confession made her wonder. When she told Jen what she'd learned, her best friend suggested that Susie check out his background before marrying him. And she did consider it. Yet she didn't because she didn't really want to know anything bad.

Sitting in the chapel, surrounded by the comforting peace and beautiful music, her mind whirled with foreboding about the marriage. *But I can't cancel it. Too many plans have already been made and too much money spent.*

"That's all stuff. It's your life that's really at stake."

Frowning, Susie looked hastily around her. *Is someone talking to me?*

The woman in front of her, as well as the man sitting near her, weren't paying any attention to her. Nor was the very old man in the front.

The voice again spoke to her soul. "You have to be true to yourself."

Startled, she cuddled into her coat. She should have been frightened or at least more curious about these strange thoughts that were penetrating her mind as though they were words spoken by someone else. But she wasn't. Somehow she felt she knew that voice and it cared about her. She looked at the baby in the manger. *I can't do that. What would everybody think?*

"That you changed your mind."

I'd disappoint them. And Frank would be furious.

"They'll all get over it."

That's what Jen said last night.

Susie could still remember when her best friend saw the real Frank. They were going to meet Jen and her boyfriend at a local restaurant, have some dinner and then take in a new movie. When they arrived, fifteen minutes late, their friends were already seated at a table. Frank immediately apologized "I'm sorry we're late. It's Susie. As usual she wasn't ready and I had to wait."

"I was late," Susie replied, "because I had to close the library. My boss went home sick."

"There you go again! With your blasted excuses!" He had grabbed her arm and squeezed it, not too much to leave a bruise but enough to hurt. "Honestly Susie, when we're married you better start to be on time. I refuse to be kept waiting."

Jennifer, whose face was growing red with anger, could hold her tongue no longer. "Frank," she said. "Maybe Susie shouldn't marry you. Because I think if she does she's going to be miserable trying to live up to your rules. And enduring your colossal rudeness!"

Frank had been so shocked that anyone would talk back to him that he sat quietly for the rest of the night. But when he got Susie alone in the car, he forbid her to have anything more to do with Jen. And that meant that her dearest friend could not even attend, let alone be in, their wedding.

Susie smiled. That was the only time she hadn't given in to him. She held her ground about Jen and it was he who finally gave in. But he refused to go out with her and her boyfriend ever again. Which was okay with Jen. She felt the same way about him. Because her girlfriend knew the truth about the real Frank, Susie had dared confess all her doubts to her. And even though Jen had bought an expensive maid-of-honor dress and hosted her biggest shower, she was very supportive. "Sus it's your life. If you don't want to live the rest of it with Frank—and who can blame you—don't. He's such a jerk," she added. "Cancel the wedding right now."

"I can't," Susie had answered.

"Why?"

"I promised Frank I'd marry him. And based on that promise, my folks have spent a fortune on this wedding. Not to mention his folks. No!" She had shaken her head so hard that her long, pale blonde hair flew across her face. "I can't go back on my word. My promise."

Jen had taken a hold of her friend and shaken her gently, then hugged her. "Oh Sus don't do it. Everyone who really loves you will understand. They want what's best for you. Your folks. Your friends. And Frank's parents certainly wouldn't want someone to marry their son who really didn't want him."

When Jen referred to her not wanting Frank, Susie had been shocked. That she, who was so mediocre compared to him, would even consider rejecting him seemed preposterous. After all, who did she think she was to consider turning down someone everyone would consider a fabulous catch? Why Frank was exactly the kind of man her sister wanted. Yet the truth was that she didn't want to spend the rest of her life struggling to please a man who would never be happy with her. No matter how hard she tried to make herself into what he wanted her to be. *I've finally realized that Frank really doesn't love me. He loves having someone to control. To boss around. But love me for me? Never!*

Knowing now that she couldn't go through with the marriage no matter what the repercussions would be, Susie looked around the chapel as though seeing it for the first time. Her gaze fastened on the glass picture of Christ healing the sick. Memories of her Bible Studies, which she had abandoned because Frank thought they were a waste of time, came back to her. She remembered the story of how Mary, Christ's mother, and his brothers had come for him while he was ministering to the crowds. They had tried to talk him into going home with them and live his life with them. But he had sent his family away and stayed, to work with the people who needed him.

You did what was right for you Jesus. What God created you to do. And I have to do that too.

"I'm glad you realize that. Because God creates everyone for a special purpose. For His purpose. And everyone is beautiful and worthy in His eyes."

Not me. He made me so plain. And boring. Not like Samantha.

"Not true. You are every bit as wonderful as your sister. Or anyone else. You have qualities that God has given only to you. They're what make you special. You must never think poorly of yourself. You are His creation. So hold your head high and have the life that you want. That you know is best for you."

I really love being with children. The library's taught me that. I still want to be a teacher.

"God planted that desire within you. And led you to that library job so you could realize it."

But I'm so worried about disappointing my family.

"I understand. I disappointed my family too."

They loved you anyway didn't they?

Susie felt her head being gently turned toward the picture of Christ hanging on the cross and the people who were grieving at his feet. "My mother was with me at the very end."

Smiling, she nodded. *Yes. Yes she was. And my family will stick by me too. I know they will.* Spreading out the fingers of her left hand, she removed her engagement ring and put it gently into her purse. As it disappeared from her sight, a delicious freedom soared through her and she felt like she could fly like an angel. She was going to be herself again - plain old Susie Porter. And while she worked to get her teaching credential, she'd teach Sunday school to the children.

She grinned at the baby Jesus at the altar. *That's right Lord. I'll be with the children. Where I belong! And I won't care how angry my family will be at me for letting go of that Good Catch.*

CHAPTER 6

◆ ◆ ◆

The Unemployed Breadwinner

Brett Montgomery slouched in the corner of a pew next to the inside aisle of the sanctuary. His hair was wet from the snow and his face was tingly from the cold.

At least it's nice and warm in here, he thought as his aching body adjusted to the hard seat. Around him, people were sitting quietly and, except for a Christmas carol automatically playing from the old organ or an occasional cough or sniffle, the church was amazingly silent.

"I could sleep here," he muttered under his breath. "Maybe I will. Because I sure can't at home." For the past few months he had added insomnia to his other troubles. It wasn't surprising that the worry that held his brain and soul in an iron grip would finally attack his ability to sleep. So now, adding to his problems was that his once energetic body was so lethargic that it moved at a snail's pace.

His shoulders curved into themselves and he closed his eyes but sleep wouldn't come. He opened them and looked at the stained glass windows, concentrating on the one of Christ carrying his cross. It reminded him of his wife, Diana. She was carrying their family now and he knew that it was a real cross for her to bear.

Until this morning, when they'd had the biggest fight of their twenty-year marriage, he hadn't realized just how frustrated she really was. It started when she was gobbling down a piece of toast before hurrying to the hospital where she worked as a nurse.

"What are you going to do today?" she asked. He noticed the forced cheerfulness in her tone.

Brett took a sip of coffee and looked up from the classified section of the newspaper. "I thought I'd stay home. It's supposed to snow a lot today."

She just glared at him. It was a look he had come to know well in the last year and a half.

"And—ah," he added, trying to appease her. "I'll probably run the vacuum. Clean up a bit around here."

Her lips snapped together in a thin line and her eyes, usually a soft brown, grew dark as she continued looking at him.

"Um—I'll also make some calls," he stammered. "Follow up on those resumes I sent out. Although I'm sure nobody's hiring now during the holidays."

That's when she exploded. "Brett Montgomery I've had it with you! With your excuses. You know very well you could find work doing something. Anything."

He braced his back against the kitchen chair as his lips also narrowed into an angry line. "Doing what?" he yelled. "Handing out shopping carts at Wal-Mart? Like you?" As soon as he spat out those words he wished, with all his heart, that he could grab them back. But it was too late.

Diana threw the toast into the sink and stomped up to him, grabbing the newspaper in front of him and throwing it across the room. "Well Mr. High and Mighty, Too Good For A Minimum

Wage Job—you would at least be bringing in some money. Any money. So I wouldn't have to do it all!"

Now, sitting in the chapel reliving the terrible fight again, he flinched. He had tried to apologize. But she refused to listen and just ran out of the house. Her final words cut his very soul. "I'm sick of you Brett. And—and I hate you."

He couldn't blame her. He wasn't any longer the man she married. And he probably never would be again.

Until eighteen months ago, he was the husband of her dreams. They had been grade school sweethearts. He could still remember, as though it was a mere minute ago, when he was first saw her. It was their first day in kindergarten. She was as tall as he was—and he was the biggest boy in the class. She also had bouncy blonde curls that he called yellow. Where other girls might have been self conscious with such height, she walked proudly and, it seemed to him, even stretched to look even longer.

Since they were the two tallest kindergartners, it was only natural that they would be attracted to each other. While he stared at her, too overcome to speak, she wasted no time getting acquainted. "I'm Diana. Who are you?"

"Ah—B- Brett. My name's Brett."

"For a boy you're cute." She leaned close to him and sniffed loudly. "You even smell good."

That did it! His heart somersaulted and from that moment on, clear through grammar and middle school, they were inseparable. In high school, they became real sweethearts who were even voted The Senior Prom King and Queen. After they both went off to separate colleges, their love affair continued. Though each had met other girls and guys who would have enabled them to enjoy the social part of school, they didn't date anyone else. Instead they telephoned every night and saw each other as much as they could. He chuckled silently. The four hundred miles that separated them were like nothing and they joked that their cars could drive automatically over those long roads because they did it so often.

When they graduated, he as a civil engineer and she as a registered nurse, they immediately married and settled in the city where he found his job because finding his was harder. She, they figured, could always find work in a hospital anywhere.

For five years they enjoyed life as a married couple with no responsibilities. They had made lots of money and spent it like crazy, with travelling, partying and generally having fun their top priority. Eventually, they decided to get serious about life and bought a house. It was a fixer upper that they rebuilt into their dream home. And then the babies came. Diana quit working to be a stay at home Mom.

First there had been Parker who had been a colicky little tyke who kept them hopping for months. Two years later Penny, the love of his life, joined them. She had been his little Princess. And she still was, even though she was a teenager now who, in his opinion, was far too young at thirteen for the make up and grown up clothes that she was wearing. He scratched his chin and frowned at the thought of how he and Diana fought about that.

Then six years after Penny's birth, when they thought they were through having children, they had Paulie. Unlike her other pregnancies, that one had been very hard on Diana. And unlike the others, she had a caesarian which prompted her to have her tubes tied after the delivery. Because of the surgery, she was in the hospital longer than she had been with Parker and Penny. When she came home, she was tired and depressed.

He had taken time off to help her. Her mother also stayed with them yet Diana wasn't happy. Nor did she even respond much to Paulie. Her doctor claimed it was just postpartum depression and gave her medication to help. And thankfully, within two weeks it did. She was her old self again, loving the kids and swooning over the baby. Brett smiled as he recalled how their life had returned to normal.

Then eighteen months ago, that wonderful life came to an abrupt end when his boss called him into his office and fired him.

One of ten engineers who had been caught in the company's downsizing, he had been taken by surprise. While it was true that he realized that the economy was bad and people were losing jobs, he felt that he would be safe. His employer was a large company with solid contracts. And he'd been there for eight years, always giving them excellent work. That they would let him go seemed preposterous.

Which was exactly what Brett told his boss, Tim, when he gave him the bad news. "How can you do this to me?" he asked. "After all I've done for this company?"

"It wasn't my idea Brett. Please believe me. In fact, I fought for you. Went over all you've done—how good you are." Tim shook his head and blinked his eyes. For a second, Brett thought his friend as well as supervisor was going to cry. Then he regained his composure. "Sorry Buddy. I couldn't budge 'em. All they see is cutting expenses." He sighed. "I expect to be next."

I hope you will be, Brett thought bitterly. Then he'd been embarrassed at his mean-spiritedness. As Tim hugged him good by, Brett knew that it wasn't his friend's fault. And he also knew that as one of the highest paid engineers, it made sense for top management to cut him if they were trying to save money.

Though shocked and disappointed, he wasn't worried. He was a good engineer with a great reputation. Obviously, other similar companies would quickly snap him up. But it didn't work that way. Like his employer, all the companies that could use his skills were experiencing the same thing. The rotten economy had ruined it for everyone, including all businesses in every industry.

He immediately set out to contact everyone he knew, sending out hundreds of resumes. While he originally didn't consider taking a job that would mean moving his family out of the home and community where they had their roots, at the end of eight months of not even an interview in his geographical area, he extended his search. Not only did he apply in other towns but even adjoining states. But in the engineering field, there was absolutely nothing.

Meanwhile they had run through their savings as well as the generous severance pay he had been given. He still remembered how secure he'd felt over that pay, believing that it would last until he found another job. But that was when he thought finding one would be a piece of cake.

Brett wriggled in his seat and stared at the people near him. They seemed like him - tired, cold and frustrated to be stuck here in this little chapel without anything to do but sit and think. He looked at the grim faced woman seated at the other end of his pew.

She looked like Diana. He raised his eyebrows then shrugged impotently. She was probably mad at her husband too.

When he finally realized that there were no jobs available in his field his wife, who hadn't worked in years but had kept her nurse's license current, went back to work. It hadn't been hard because unlike other industries, hospitals always needed nurses, especially if they were willing to take unpopular shifts like Christmas and other holidays.

That's really when things started to go bad between Diana and me, he thought. When she started working and I became Mr. Mom, the househusband. Brett had never needed to do anything around the house other than mow their lawn on the rare occasion when the gardener didn't show up. Now his wife expected him to vacuum, dust, mop floors, wash dishes and even the laundry.

She'd had to show him how to do all those domestic chores. And he hadn't liked it. "You know I'll be working again soon," he said. "So don't get too hung up on making me a maid." He'd smiled and even chuckled when he'd said that, trying to keep the message light while still getting his point across.

But Diana didn't find it amusing. Her mouth tightened and her eyes grew narrow and dark. It was an expression he was getting to know well. "Since I'm working ten hour shifts and you're not working at all," she sarcastically emphasized the last four words in clipped syllables, "I should think you'd be willing to help me." What she didn't say but he knew she thought was "It's the least you can do".

He started doing the household chores, which included driving the kids to and from school. That was the most embarrassing of all as the other parents, who were picking up their children, were all stay at home mothers like his wife used to be. By then, everyone knew that Diana had gone back to work because he was a loser without a job.

That's when he decided that maybe he had better switch careers. He went to the first job fair he found and been shocked to discover that there were over three hundred people, just like him, desperately looking for work.

There were few employers offering real jobs with a steady paycheck and benefits.

But there were many offering commission only sales positions. A life insurance company was recruiting agents and one of their managers stopped him as he was walking by their booth. "Hi there!" A tall man in a navy suit, white shirt and red and blue striped tie said. "You look exactly like the kind of man we're looking for."

Before Brett knew it, the man had him in his booth and was singing the praises of his company and how great it was to be an insurance agent.

Brett figured he might as well give that career a try, as there wasn't anything else available for him. His wife was surprisingly encouraging even when she learned he'd have to spend a few hundred dollars for classes to prepare him for an insurance license and errors and omissions insurance to cover any law suits he might experience.

Remembering when he had purchased life insurance several years ago, Brett had been amazed that it had been so difficult to get into the profession. The whole process had taken a couple months before he could even get started. And before too long he knew it wasn't for him.

But he did try. Showed up at the office every day as soon as he took the kids to school, made his prospecting calls, followed up on leads and attended every training that the company offered. Since he'd performed in Community Theatre until he lost his job, he was good at memorization so he had no trouble learning the exact words of his presentations and the responses to peoples' many objections. Yet though his bosses helped him as much as they could, after several months his sales were still unacceptably low. In fact, he hadn't even earned enough to pay his car expenses. So once again, he was forced to face some more unpleasant facts. He just wasn't cut out to be a salesman, to talk to complete strangers in their homes among their kids and animals.

And the part he hated the most was the feeling that he was intruding on people's privacy in order to sell them something they probably couldn't afford—even if they did need it. *I wanted to tell them to put the money they'd pay on a premium into a savings account so they'd have money if they lost their job.* He chuckled. *Some salesman I was!*

Eventually he just stopped going to the office and the meetings. And no one from the insurance company even bothered to call him.

Once again he returned to being a full time househusband. That's when he discovered the home supply business. There, through the internet and catalogues, folks could buy the stuff they use everyday cheaper than it cost them in the stores.

He had been introduced to the business by Tim, his old boss, who had been laid off two months after Brett. Like him, he hadn't been able to find work either.

"The real opportunity," Tim explained, "is in signing up your family and people you know to sell the products too. Then you make money on all their sales."

At first Brett, afraid of another failure, was skeptical. "I don't know," he said. "I'm not the salesman type. I bombed when I tried to sell life insurance."

His friend waved away his concern. "Well of course you would. Selling insurance is probably the hardest thing in the world to sell. After all, who wants to buy something that suggests a person will die. But this," he grinned broadly. "This is a no brainer. After all, everybody buys laundry detergent, dishwashing soap, garbage bags and a whole bunch of other stuff they absolutely have to have in order to live." Tim, who had only been in the business himself for two weeks, was so excited that Brett decided that maybe it would be a great way to make money. So he spent fifty dollars he didn't have and attended meetings where people who had been with the company for years told how they were making six figure incomes working only a few hours a week.

He even dragged Diana to a few meetings and together, they started doing everything they were told to do to start making all that money. But it turned out to be much harder than it looked. He chuckled cynically as he recalled how their friends practically ran from them whenever they started talking about their business opportunity.

Brett began massaging the sides of his forehead as an ache started to pound little hammers behind his brows. Eventually that, like insurance, flopped too and they were stuck with a bunch of products they'd never use. He and Tim, who was equally disappointed in the business, finally took it all to a swap meet and sold it five cents on the dollar.

After that fiasco, he was now back to where he was when he was first laid off. Only money was tighter than ever. Diana's salary, even with her overtime, still didn't come close to what Brett's income had been.

Then two months ago, with the holidays approaching, his wife had also taken a part time job with their neighborhood Wal-Mart. He had been horrified—not so much because she'd be pushing herself harder which couldn't be good for her physically—but because now all their neighbors, many of their friends and even people who had seen him perform in the theatre would know that Brett Montgomery was such a loser that his wife had to hold down two jobs to support the family.

"Because I couldn't, or wouldn't," he whispered to himself. "That's what Diana thinks." After the fight this morning she had shamed him sufficiently so that he threw on a sweater and some slacks and an old coat and gone to fast food restaurants that paid minimum wages to try to find a job.

It took him five visits to places that sold hot dogs, chicken, donuts, gourmet coffee and tacos before he finally landed a job at a hamburger joint. Brett had been interviewed by a young kid who still had acne. That he would have to answer to this infant manager depressed him so much that he felt like vomiting. But he needed a job so he took it.

He was to start tomorrow and even work Christmas Day. It would serve Diana right to not have him home on Christmas. But he knew that would be okay with her because she'd made it clear that she hated him anyway.

He had taken the humiliating job at a Burgers 'N Buns to show her that he wasn't as lazy as she thought. That he was willing to lower himself to work at a menial job if it would make her happy. But he hadn't thought that he'd ever be doing anything that menial. He sighed. And taking orders from a snot nose kid! That would be the final insult.

He stared again at the picture of Christ carrying his cross. He already knew this awful job would be his cross to bear. He blinked back the sudden tears that were filling his eyes. There was one good thing about that lousy job, he thought. The Burgers 'N Buns where he'd be working wasn't anywhere near his house but actually just down the street from where he was sitting now in the chapel. So hopefully none of his neighbors or anybody he knew would see him.

His lips twisted at the snobbish thought. He couldn't help it. He had worked hard to get his education. And he had been a wonderful engineer and a good employee. It wasn't fair that he was now reduced to slinging hamburgers.

He then looked at the picture of Christ healing the sick and working his miracles, He and Diana used to teach Bible Studies about Jesus when he was working. And they had joined prayer sessions when he first lost his job. They had been great believers in God, knowing with a certainty that if they just had enough faith—no more than the size of a tiny mustard seed—that they could move a mountain. Even if that mountain was finding a new job in a down economy.

Where's your miracle God? Where's your help? His wet eyes were aching hollows as he stared at the portrayal of Christ. *Where are you?*

"I'm here. With you. As I've always been."

Brett jumped and looked around. For a second he thought someone had spoken to him. But no one was paying him any attention. *I must be imagining things. I thought I heard someone talk to me.*

"You did." The voice was clear as it bypassed his ears and spoke only to his mind.

Who—who are you?

"Who did you just talk to? In your thoughts?"

Brett shook his head and frowned. The picture of Christ with the crowds seemed to grow larger and more vivid. *I was wondering why God hasn't helped me. Led me to a job.*

"I did. Today."

His heart fell. *I mean a real job. Like I used to have. So Diana wouldn't have to work. And we'd be like we used to be.*

"I didn't want you to be like you used to be."

Brett's mouth fell open and he shivered. This couldn't be happening. He must be losing his mind.

"You and Diana had become complacent snobs. Not grateful for what you had."

We gave money to the church. Taught a Bible Study.

"You voted against city bonds that would have helped the schools and built shelters for the homeless. You ignored the toy drives at Christmas. And even forgot to put canned goods out at your mailbox for the postal workers to pick up and give to the hungry."

We—ah—I wasn't interested in paying more taxes.

"Taxes help do my work."

I guess I never thought about that.

"Brett, you got to the point that you didn't notice the hurting world around you. Now you know."

Brett took a deep, jagged breath as his soul spoke. *Yeah. That's for sure. Now I'm one of them!*

"Not quite. You're still luckier than most. And now you even have a job."

If you can call it that. It's really an insult.

"Only if you let it be. You know, the people who came to me for miracles might've wanted more than I gave them. But they took what they got and, for the most part, made the best of their lives."

You want me to do that too?

"Yes."

But it's so humiliating. To flip hamburgers at a Burgers 'N Buns. To answer to a kid.

"It's an honest job. And you might learn quite a bit from that kid."

How can I face my wife? My kids? People I know?

"With pride in knowing you are willing to do anything to feed your family. And that you are doing this with faith in me, knowing that I have put you exactly where you need to be."

Irritation pounded Brett's mind. This was not the miracle he had hoped God would give him.

The voice held a smile. "Ah My Son, miracles come in all kinds of packages. And most don't start out looking like much at all."

Suddenly, a miraculous warm light filled him, making him lighter and restoring his energy. The anger, bitterness and embarrassment flowed out of him as his body warmed to a renewed optimism unlike anything he had ever felt before. That positive feeling, he knew, was real because that whole experience of having a two-sided conversation with His Lord, which seemed to take only seconds, was very real. How Brett could be sure of that he didn't know. But what he did know, with the same certainty that the seat under him was hard, was that he truly had heard the voice of His Heavenly Father.

Joy consumed him as his soul filled with renewed hope and his heart soared. Is it possible that this job will turn out to be a good thing, he wondered.

He laughed out loud, interrupting the quiet around him as he realized that he no longer cared what people would think of him and his new job. He didn't even like hamburgers. But he would honor God by being the best burger flipper Burgers 'N Buns ever employed. And he'd keep doing it until God came up with something better for him to do.

CHAPTER 7

The Bitter Housewife

Isabelle Franklin glowered at the people entering the chapel as she struggled out of her big, black quilted coat. She had practically frozen to death outside and now she was roasting as the church grew warmer with more bodies.

Isabelle's three large shopping bags filled the seats and floor directly beside her and she straddled the biggest one with her heavily booted feet. "Nobody but a complete idiot would be out in this weather doing last minute shopping," she whispered as she loosened a green crocheted scarf from her head and fluffed her thick, salt and pepper hair. She figured that she must look like a big bear in all her clothes. Her nose, which she hated because it was no more than a button between her two puffy cheeks, wrinkled disdainfully. *A graying bear, that's what I am.*

In an effort to lift her spirits, she ran her hands over the outsides of each of her bags. Feeling the shapes of their contents she smiled. Even in this terrible weather she had excelled in the shopping. But then she always did. With four children, five if she was to count her daughter-in-law as one of her children, plus a husband and assorted other relatives to shop for, there seemed to be no end to buying Christmas presents. But that she had waited until the last minute to buy much of it was certainly not typical of her usually well organized self.

She couldn't believe how she had allowed time to get away from her. What with the decorating, cooking, cleaning and her problem with Louis, she had fallen terribly behind.

Tears started sneaking into her eyes and she blinked them back so rapidly that her eyelids resembled fluttering hummingbird wings. How could she possibly get through the holidays knowing what Louis planned to do when they were over?

He had dropped his bomb two weeks ago on a Sunday afternoon when she was decorating the family room for Christmas. She had innocently made a comment that she never dreamed would create such turmoil in her marriage. Struggling to put together the eight-foot artificial tree whose branches all needed to be individually placed into the base and fluffed up to look real, she had turned to her husband, who was reading a book in his leather recliner. "Louis," she said. "We really need to add on to this room. It's just too small."

Lowering his book, he pushed his glasses down on his nose and looked around him. He was a big man, over six feet tall with a broad back that carried forty extra pounds. He owned a small chain of hardware stores and since Sunday was his only day off, he jealously guarded the leisure it offered. Now he was studying the room as if seeing it for the first time, which was ridiculous since he'd spent a portion of his every day in it for the past twenty years. "It looks big enough to me," he said quietly.

Isabelle shook her head. "Not really. It's quite small. And I always realize it when I put up the tree. Then we're really crowded."

"I have the perfect solution," he said as he put a bookmark in his book and slammed it shut. "Get a smaller tree."

She laughed. "Louis really! That's not the answer."

His face was serious, his eyes small dots as they peered at her from above his glasses. "Yes it is Isabelle." His voice started to rise. "In fact it's a great idea. If the tree makes the room crowded, scale down the tree. Because I'm not going to remodel one more thing on this house. Not now. Not ever."

Having just climbed off the tall ladder after arranging the branches on the top, she stopped at his words. Tentatively, she reached for the ornament that their last child, sixteen year old Angelique, had made in kindergarten and caressed it. "You're kidding, right?" She went over to her husband and sat on the sofa next to his chair.

He shook his head. "Not at all. I'm sick of constantly having a part of this house torn apart while you remodel."

She put down Angelique's paper Santa face with the cotton ball beard and pouted angrily. "I can't believe I'm hearing this! I thought you liked what we've done. To make the house nice."

"Nice Isabelle? You've made this house much more than just nice. It's a blasted showcase."

Indignation crawled up her spine, straightening her back. "That's bad?" she shouted. "That I've made a beautiful home for you? For the kids?"

He raised then lowered his big hands. "No. That's not bad. But—but you've gone overboard. Just like you always do. About everything. And I'm tired." His voice became very low and she had to lean forward to hear him. "I'm just so very, very tired."

A dark shadow crossed her face, denting her brow. Her husband, who she thought she knew as well as she knew herself, was frightening her with his strange talk. "Oh Louis," she said. "I'm sorry. I didn't realize you don't feel well."

He gave her a small, melancholy smile. "I feel fine. I'm just tired of your constant fussing. Over the house. Which never pleases you. And the kids. Who don't do anything right." He shook his head as she stared at him. "And now you've got a daughter-in-law to complain about. God! It never ends!"

Anger welled up within her. "Well," she snapped, "I didn't know I was such a terrible wife!"

He took off his glasses and rubbed the bridge of his nose. "You're not Isabelle. Not really. It's just me. I'm just not happy with my life anymore." He forced himself out of the chair and it occurred to her that he moved like an old man. He looked down at her. His face was a mask of sadness. "After the holidays I'm going to get away for awhile. Take a vacation of sorts."

She smiled. "Good. We need one. Laurette can stay here and take care of Angelique."

He shook his head. "No Isabelle. This isn't a vacation for us. Only me. I want to get away alone. To think." Then he had walked out of the room. Later he'd left to go to his office, which was something he never did on Sunday.

For the rest of the day she sat silently on the sofa, the tree and decorating left undone. Louis had been like a stranger to her. As alien as a man from another planet.

While she sat staring into the empty family room, her mind flashed onto the scenes of their life together; trying to understand what possible basis he had for these awful complaints about her. They had met when they both worked part-time at Anderson's Hardware store. A freshman at the community college, she worked twenty hours a week as bookkeeper while Louis, whose main job was in his uncle's contracting business, filled in as a salesman for the store when his uncle's work was slow. It was a cost effective arrangement for old man Anderson and it helped Isabelle and Louis too.

At first they had simply been colleagues who spoke very little to each other as they conscientiously went about their tasks. Then one evening he offered to take her home when her car wouldn't start. She could have called her father to get her. Later she would claim that she didn't know why she hadn't because she wasn't the least bit attracted to Louis. She admitted that he was nice enough but he just wasn't her type.

Though her plain looks had never attracted them, her type was dark haired jocks and Louis was a tall, overweight red head. But when they stopped for pie and coffee on their way home and started talking, they discovered that they had a lot in common. Each was the oldest of three siblings, loved Dalmatians, hated tomatoes but liked tomato sauce, disliked seafood, broccoli and pistachio ice cream and would rather read or watch television than go dancing or to big, loud parties. And Louis had made her laugh. She had always been so serious but he had a wonderful way of looking at things—even bad things—and turning them into something funny.

Sitting alone in the family room amidst the Christmas decorations, she wondered where his humor had gone. "When was the last time he joked?" she asked the bare tree. "And when last did we have a good laugh together?" Tears pooled in her eyes and started to spill over. She dabbed at them. "Oh Louis," she cried. "What's happened to us? We used to be so good together."

After that first evening in the pie shop, they were inseparable. Three months later they eloped. They'd done it against her parents' wishes as they thought their daughter and the first boyfriend she really ever had didn't know each other long enough to get married. They were confident that they didn't need a long courtship to know what they had realized that first night—they were true soul mates.

Shortly after that Dick Anderson offered Louis a full time job as the hardware store's manager. He took it because it paid benefits. Isabelle remained the part time bookkeeper, but soon dropped out of school. Louis, who had also been taking a few classes at the college, quit too, claiming that he was too busy at the store to study.

Two years later Lawrence was born and Anderson sold the store to them for a small down payment, a low interest rate and monthly payments that were easy to make. "I like you kids, "the old man had said. "And I want you to have a chance in life. My little store'll do that for you."

Since he had no heirs, there was a clause in the contract that if the purchase price wasn't paid by the time Anderson died, they would no longer have to pay the loan. At the time they hadn't realized, when he offered the store to them, that Dick knew he was dying. He only lived a year after that and Isabelle and Louis got the bargain of the century.

They both worked in the store, taking Lawrence with them. Two years later, with Isabelle's perfect planning, their first daughter Laurette, came along. During that time they had expanded the store and built two new ones in growing suburbs.

With three Anderson Hardwares, as they had kept the business's original name out of respect for their benefactor, Dick Anderson, and two children, the couple became extremely busy. "But we still found time for each other," she remembered. They always had their weekly date night, even if it was no more than going out for coffee and pie. Or going to the shooting range to enjoy their shared hobby of guns.

She blinked and wiggled her foot so hard that one of her bags tipped over. She frowned as she righted it. When had they stopped their date night? With a start she realized she couldn't remember the last time they'd gone out together. *My Word! We have grown apart! But then we've been awful busy.*

The years had flown by. Four more stores and two more children were added to their lives. Two years after Laurette, Isabelle planned another baby and Luke was born. Only Angelique had surprised Isabelle, coming along six years later. Because the nurse in the delivery room called her an angel and Louis was sick of giving all the kids a name beginning with the letter L, they had named her Angelique.

Isabelle was busier than ever. After Luke's birth she had stopped working in the business and had concentrated on becoming the consummate homemaker and mother. When they decided they could afford to buy a house after their third child, Isabelle became obsessed with finding the right one. But no new ones being built in young suburbs or older homes in established neighborhoods came close to what she wanted for her family. *Was it my fault nothing fit us? I wasn't going to waste our hard earned money on something less than perfect.*

Eventually Louis agreed to build their home. It took almost a year for Isabelle to find the right vacant lot and another year to build the house, whose plans were changed twice during the building process. But after they moved in and had all the kids Isabelle realized that the house already needed upgrading. She assumed Louis had understood that as he certainly acted like he agreed. A pool and huge game room were added off the remodeled kitchen, the master bedroom was expanded, all the windows were replaced with window seats and closets were redesigned with drawers and shelves and rotating shoe racks. Every child had his or her own room, perfectly decorated and redecorated as the child's interests and Isabelle's tastes changed.

The house seemed to be a constant work in progress, never completely finished.

Sitting alone that Sunday afternoon, Isabelle could understand why the constant redecorating would frustrate her husband. Yet it had all been necessary. Their family was constantly changing and the house had to change with it. For the life of her she couldn't figure out why Louis didn't seem to get that.

What she didn't like to admit but did as she sat there all by herself was that she frequently grew bored with her house and wanted to change it, particularly if she saw something in a magazine or belonging to a friend who sported a room or a look that appealed to her. Then she had to have it too.

But the house wasn't the only thing her husband had complained to her about. He had also hurled mean accusations at her regarding her relationship with her children. *Louis said I think the kids don't do anything right. That's certainly not true. I just encourage them to be the best they can be. And be better than anyone else.*

It started when Lawrence was just a baby. She had devoured every childcare book she could find and among them was a book explaining how tiny babies could be taught to read before they were two. Even though her husband thought she was crazy, she did everything the book told her to do, showing little Lawrence flash cards of the alphabet before he could hardly focus his eyes, playing tapes of Shakespeare and classical music. When he was two he was enrolled in an experimental school designed to make him a genius. Extolling only academics, the school wouldn't allow their little students to play with ordinary toys like balls and stuffed animals. So Isabelle followed suit with her son.

Eventually, when her first born showed behavior problems, she had to admit that maybe she had gone a bit overboard with him. Perhaps Louis had been right. Her shoving school at him so early had definitely turned him into a lousy student and a problem child. She sighed. At least now, as a married adult, Lawrence was doing well working for his father.

Laurette, her precious first daughter, was a diminutive little beauty. How she and Louis, who were both big boned and overweight, could produce such a petite child was a mystery. Then her mother reminded her that her French grandmother was small and beautiful. *Obviously Laurette took after her. So of course I had to build on that. Which is why I entered her in those pageants.*

Little Laurette won her first beauty pageant at three months—Newborn Supreme Queen. Through the years Isabelle gave her dancing and singing lessons so she'd excel at the talent part of the competitions and hired a "pageant" coach to teach her how to walk and smile at the judges plus make-up and hair stylists who accompanied them to all the pageants. Louis accused Isabelle of living vicariously through Laurette. And it was partly true.

88

Isabelle had never been pretty like her daughter. So it was only normal that she would want her child to be what she had never been able to do. "What," she had asked her husband, "was so wrong with that?"

As she grew older, Laurette began to measure her worth solely by her wins. When she didn't win the top honor, even though she was still beautiful and talented, she fell into depressions that grew more severe as the pageants became more competitive and important. Finally, when she lost the Junior Miss Pageant at thirteen, she tried to commit suicide by slitting her wrists. Only their Dalmatian, Bessie, saved her by barking so hard at her bedroom door that Isabelle finally checked on her.

That terrible incident brought everything to a stop. The psychiatrist Isabelle and Louis saw at the hospital told them that if they didn't let Laurette quit the pageants, she'd just try to kill herself again. And she would eventually succeed. The memory of those awful days when her own child refused to see her cut Isabelle's heart into what felt like strips. She had never, ever dreamed that her daughter didn't want to be in the pageants. Isabelle had always asked her before they would go to one if she really wanted to do it and she always answered with a firm yes and one of her beauty queen dimpled smiles.

Later Isabelle learned Laurette only wanted to please her. From that moment on, and even now, Isabelle spoiled Laurette, doing everything she could to make her happy.

Now, as a hymn about Joy swirled around her in the chapel, Isabelle automatically reached into the shopping bag by her right arm. Her fingers closed around the velvet box that was Laurette's special present. It was a diamond pendant shaped like a crooked heart with Laurette's birthstone, a tear drop sapphire, dangling in the center. It was designed by Sheba, a famous star of movies and music and all the young women wanted one. Every jewelry store was sold out. Except for one Isabelle discovered after calling all the jewelry stores in the city for the fifth time that week. They had just gotten a return that morning. The wrong birthstone for the first buyer was perfect for Isabelle who bought it over the phone, then dropped everything to hurry out in the terrible weather to pick it up.

But Laurette was worth it. She had graduated with a degree in fashion design and was designing her own bridal gown for her wedding in June. And the sketches and fabric swatches indicated that it would be breathtaking. Even Isabelle, who wasn't very fashion conscious, realized that. Her own figure had become too chunky to be fashionable and frankly, she never felt she could take time to fuss with herself.

Now with Louis acting so strange maybe she had been wrong. Her eyes stung with a weary bitterness. She couldn't help that she hadn't kept herself up better. Instead she had put her family first. Not that that's worth anything, she thought angrily.

She checked another bag and sighed. She hoped Luke would like the Jade carved chess set she found for him in the jewelry store where she got Laurette's heart. It would make a wonderful add on gift to his major one of matching leather luggage. Ever since he was little, her third child's interests were all cerebral and though she tried not to push him, she couldn't help but enroll him in the special school and clubs that challenged his awesome mind. Being the bright son she had tried to make Lawrence into, Luke was so smart that he had skipped grades. Which she had approved of even though Louis had been against it.

"You're cheating him of a childhood. And every kid needs one," Louis had argued.

"I don't agree with that," Isabelle retorted. "And neither do the school people. They think it'd be terrible to hold him back."

In the end Louis did what he always did and gave in. Fighting Isabelle, he often said, was just too much work.

So Luke ended up graduating from high school at fourteen, two years before his older sister and with his eighteen year old brother. It had been awkward and Isabelle did have to admit, though it killed her, that her young son looked very small and frail next to his more mature classmates. But she was very proud of him and figured that Louis was too.

Luke immediately went onto the best university in the state. "But he didn't last the year," Isabelle sighed. Louis had been right. He had been too emotionally immature. Her son ended up working for Louis until he could discover what he really wanted to do. He finally made that discovery when he entered his first chess tournament.

He had loved it. For a while Luke hadn't earned enough to make his expenses but they didn't care. He was happy. That's all that mattered to them. Now he was actually earning enough money to support himself. So the jade chess set would be perfect for him. Although if Louis knew how much she paid for it, he would have a fit. Another fit, she thought grimly, since he was having so many of them lately.

When Angelique came along, Isabelle had decided to back off from being what her husband called a stage mother. Yet when the little girl was only two it was obvious that her small body was more flexible than most children's. *In Toddler Tumbling she showed such promise. Of course I had to put her in gymnastics. It was a must with her talent. And she loved it. She really did. I was sure of that.*

Until the training switched from a fun hobby to Olympic preparations. Then Angelique's life became one of constant work. And she didn't like it. Had, in fact, started hating it. Isabelle had told Angelique that she could quit if she wanted to. But she also stated that she felt it would be a pity to quit after all the years she'd devoted to training. Her youngest who she thought she had such a close relationship with had taken her unhappiness right to her father who immediately cancelled everything and confronted Isabelle with an anger she had never seen before.

"Angellique's through with gymnastics. She never wants to see another balance beam or floor mat again."

"But she's worked so hard."

"She hates it."

"To quit now."

"She has no life." He glared at her from over his glasses and tightened his jaw. "Let her be like everyone else. NORMAL!"

But she wasn't normal. She was so much above everyone. Isabelle shook her head. *It was a pity that Angelique gave it all up.*

So now her teen-age daughter just played, went to school and became a cheerleader. Isabelle had immediately wanted to give her special cheer leading lessons in order to give her a head start on the competition. But once again Louis went ballistic.

"Absolutely not!" he yelled. "Leave her alone. Let her get it on her own."

And she had. Isabelle was so proud. And surprised.

She grinned as she thought about her kids. They had all done well. *I don't know why Louis thinks they don't please me. They do. All of them. Except maybe for Lawrence who made a poor choice in a wife. He could've done so much better* She had told Louis just that the first time she met Lupe.

"What's wrong with her?" Louis asked. "I think she's nice. And cute."

"Well she seems nice enough. And I suppose she's cute. But Louis, she's not like us."

"What do you mean? Not like us?"

She rolled her yes. "You know. Not our kind."

He laughed. "Unless I've missed something she's human. Like us. Our kind."

"You know she's different. Her race. Her culture."

He waved away her words. "Join the twenty first century Isabelle. Those things don't matter any more."

She stiffened indignantly. "Well they should. Marriage is hard enough without having background differences."

"What counts is the kind of person she is. And she looks

to be a fine young lady with high morals and a good mind. An educated mind," he emphasized.

"I think you should talk to Lawrence. Tell him to consider their differences before he gets in any deeper."

"I will not. I have faith in our son's good sense."

Eventually she took it upon herself to talk to her son. She hadn't been able to help it. All she'd really wanted was for Lawrence to be sure about what he was doing and anticipate how society could cause him and Lupe problems with their interracial marriage. All that conversation accomplished was a rift between her and her first born that lasted until Louis got them together and forced them to make up. It took place one month before the young couple's wedding, which had been totally planned without Isabelle's input. She had behaved herself about not trying to take over the wedding. But she had thrown a magnificent bridal shower and rehearsal dinner that was far better than the wedding reception Lupe's parents gave.

Isabelle fidgeted in the pew and moved the shopping bags to give her legs more room. I thought everything was fine. Lupe and I were even warming to each other. Then Lawrence dropped his bomb.

Just a few weeks ago, he visited his parents alone. It was the day after Thanksgiving. "Mom. Dad. I want to tell you what Lupe and I have decided about the holidays. Specifically Christmas."

She turned from the kitchen counter where she was cutting day old pumpkin pie. "What do you mean? What's to decide?"

She could see Lawrence visibly gulp. It reminded her of when he was little, trying to tell a lie.

"We feel since we both have families that want us to be with them on important holidays that we should be very fair. If we spend one major holiday with one family, then we do the next one with the other."

Louis nodded as his glasses slipped down on his nose. "Makes sense."

Isabelle bridled "Just what does this mean? To us? And Christmas?"

"Well Mom since we spent Thanksgiving with you, we're going to spend Christmas day with Lupe's family. Then next year we'll be with them Thanksgiving and you Christmas. That way it'll be fair for everyone."

Isabelle's stomach churned. "I don't believe it! How can you think this is fair? You know what Christmas means to me. To us!"

"I know Mom. But it means a lot to Lupe's family too. This is what we're going to do." He looked at his father with desperation oozing from his eyes.

"Sounds fair to me," Louis said. "After all Isabelle we can't expect to always have the kids with us."

"I think this is just awful. And selfish of Lupe to take you away from your family on the most important day of the year." Suddenly Isabelle remembered that old poem that went around between mothers of sons…a daughter's a daughter all of her life, a son's a son 'til he takes a wife. That certainly seemed to be coming true with her son. And never in a million years would she have expected it. Lawrence had always been so devoted to her—before Lupe.

But now he was sticking up for his bride. "It isn't just Lupe's idea," Lawrence said. "It's mine too. We're trying to consider everyone."

Isabelle started to cry. "When are we supposed to celebrate with you? Or are we?"

"How about Christmas Eve?"

She sniffed. "We don't celebrate then. Only on Christmas day."

"Well we can start," Louis said, his voice cheerful. "We can celebrate both Christmas Eve and Day. Celebrate twice." He grinned as Lawrence looked at him gratefully. "Have twice the fun!"

"And twice the work," she retorted. "For me of course."

"No Mom!" Lawrence quickly said. "Lupe said she'd bring the dinner. Since we won't cook on Christmas and she knows you will, she thought it'd be easier on you. That way you can rest and enjoy yourself."

Isabelle glared at him. "I won't need Lupe's food. I'll cook something myself if I decide to do this. Right now I'm not sure. Maybe we'll just skip Christmas all together. Since some of us will be missing."

When he heard that, Louis quickly led Lawrence outside before more could be said.

Later my dear husband came back in and told me off. Said I was being stubborn and hateful. Even unloving. She smirked at the memory. *That had been easy for him to say. He never did anything for Christmas except show up to hand out the presents I bought and eat food I cooked.*

She looked around the chapel, taking in the nativity set, cross and stained glass pictures. Now that she'd had a chance to rest a bit, she had to admit that this was a pretty little place in a simple, well worn sort of way. Certainly it encouraged one to think, if her fellow visitor's serious faces were any indication.

She bit the lower corner of her mouth as anger once again engulfed her. *Louis has his nerve. Attacking me! Saying he was tired and needed a vacation. Well if anyone needs a vacation it's me.*

After Louis told her that he refused to expand the family room and that he was going away after the holidays, Isabelle felt ill. When he finally came back from the office that Sunday and for the days since then she'd hardly spoken to him and he was equally silent around her. It wasn't that they were rude or even cold toward each other. In fact they were overly polite, even continuing to sleep together though barely touching. She had, of course, immediately suspected that he was having an affair. But after checking his clothes, his Day Timer and receipts she decided that wasn't the case.

Maybe Louis is just tired. I know how he feels. I'm tired too. Of doing everything for everybody. Of having no time for me.

She had once had dreams too. Personal things that she had wanted to accomplish in her life. Then she'd married and had a family and given herself totally to them. She'd never regretted it until now when she realized that nothing she had done seemed to be appreciated.

Away In The Manger was playing from the organ and Isabelle swallowed down a new batch of tears. That song always reminded her of her children when they were babies and needed her.

Her face drooped as she again considered her husband. *What if Louis decides to divorce me? What will I do? I've never worked except for him. And I don't look good anymore. Been too busy to keep myself up. My Word! I'll end up homeless. Living on the street.*

"No you won't."

Isabelle's eyes grew wide. *Who's that?*

Shaking, she scrutinized the people sitting near her. There were only two—a man at the end of her pew with a sad face and a young girl behind her who reminded her of her daughters. Neither of them were looking at her, let alone speaking out loud.

She silently repeated her question. *Who is that?*

"Who do you think it is? You're in a church. My house."

She was shaking so hard that she had to grasp the edge of the pew to keep from collapsing. *God?*

"Yes."

I must be losing my mind. She nodded. Yes. That was it. She was finally having a nervous breakdown from all the stress.

"You're not crazy. And you're not having a breakdown. You've just finally been forced to face your life. So you can fix it."

Tears burst from Isabelle's eyes and her little nose began to run. Not having any tissue, she wiped it with her hand. *I don't know what to do. Nobody loves me. I try so hard to be a good wife and mother. But they all hate me.*

"No they don't. They love you. But you do frustrate them with your overbearing attention."

Louis's going to divorce me. I know it!

"No he's not. He really is just tired. And he wants to decide what to do with the stores."

Her mind jerked to attention. *What about the stores?*

"He's got a buyer for them."

He never told me.

"Because you'd immediately take charge. Make the decision for him."

Her shoulders slumped as she looked at her lap. *I've always taken over. Because no one else would do it right.* She shivered in disgust at how that last word proclaimed her perfectionism attitude. She had always believed that no one could do anything as well as she did. So she had just taken on everything herself. Then she wouldn't have to see their mediocre jobs. And become impatient because they wouldn't move as fast as she could. Now she was starting to wonder if maybe that was the wrong way to live.

She stared at the picture of Christ coming out of the water when John baptized him. Baptismal means a new beginning. She sighed. *How I wish I could have a new beginning.*

"You can."

"How?" her tired mind asked.

"Revive your lost dreams. Do something that you really love to do. Just for you." The words spoke with a kind authority that caressed her soul.

Immediately her heart wrapped around the long ago vision of a tearoom where she could bake her pastries, brew her teas and create amazing sandwiches and salads. She had pictured it occasionally through all the years of chauffeuring kids to activities.

She even knew how she'd decorate it with big, live plants, bright flowers and comfortable white wicker furniture. It would be an oasis of peace and beauty where harried women, like her, could go for an hour or two of calming rejuvenation.

She smiled at the memory of the bridal shower she'd given for Lawrence's Lupe. Until now she hadn't realized that she had decorated and served foods like she would offer if she had a tearoom.

My tearoom's always been with me.

"Then open one."

I can't. The children...

"The children," the voice interrupted, "are grown. They don't need your constant attention. Don't want it."

But Louis needs me. He wouldn't want me to do it.

"He'd love for you to do it. To have something that's wholly yours."

But if he sells the stores, what will he do? How will we live?

"He'll make a lot of money on the sale. More than enough to live on and open your tearoom. And he's already got a job lined up.

What?

"He wants to go on the road. Sell hardware supplies to stores like his. After all the years cooped up in the office he yearns for freedom to move around."

Isabelle's heart plummeted. Her husband hadn't told her any of this. And they used to tell each other everything. *Why didn't he tell me all this?*

"Because you'd throw up a lot of negatives and..."

Lawrence! Her mind cried, interrupting even the voice of God. *What will happen to his job if Louis sells the business? Where will he go?*

"Lawrence is going to join the police department. He's already passed the pre-employment tests. He starts January second."

Her mouth fell open and she covered it with her hand. *Oh no!*

That's too dangerous! He could be killed. She would absolutely forbid it. As soon as she got home she'd call him and really put her foot down.

"There you go again Isabelle. Trying to run a life that's not your own."

That's bad? To be a mother concerned for her child?

"No. What's bad is being a controlling mother who keeps her children from doing what they want."

Lawrence could be killed. It's a dangerous job.

"He knows that. But it's what he wants. It's his passion just as the tearoom is yours."

Suddenly Isabelle felt her coat and bags huddle around her as if she were being cradled in a cocoon. It felt like the very arms of God were hugging her even as confusion tightly held her mind. She and Louis had been sporadic churchgoers. Yet they did believe in God. And she did say her prayers every night before she went to sleep. And since Louis had been so hateful, she had even doubled up on them lately. So maybe it was God talking to her.

I don't know. This is all so confusing. I don't understand.

"Understand this Isabelle. I've created everyone with certain dreams and desires that will fulfill their lives and serve me. Lawrence will touch many lives for me as a cop. Louis will too when he gets on the road. And you'll be amazed at what you can do for me in your tearoom."

Again she looked at Christ's baptismal scene. Maybe a new beginning would be possible for her and for them. She didn't know how all that would happen. She folded her hands and did the only thing she knew to do. That she'd been taught as a little girl in Sunday School to do whenever she had a problem or a request for her Heavenly Father. Funny, she thought. *I've been so busy being a mother I've forgotten that I do have a Heavenly Father.*

She started her prayer with a tiny whisper. "Dear God. I am

most willing to take that new life you're going to give me. And the new lives you're going to give Louis and our children. And I promise—I do promise—that I'll try not to interfere and be judgmental. No matter what they decide to do. But God, you will have to help me. Please."

A plaque with a Bible verse that had hung in a long forgotten Sunday School class she had attended came back to her.

"With God all things are possible," it said.

She giggled. "Yes God I know. And," she winked at the cross, "I'm counting on it."

CHAPTER 8

◆ ❖ ◆

The Vengeful Divorcee

Darlene Dexter crossed her legs and shook her right foot in the air over the floor. Fury whirled through her as she looked at the people scattered around her in the little chapel's pews. In spite of her upset over getting beaten again in court and this blizzard that had sabotaged her ability to leave New Stockford's wretched downtown, her writer's curiosity took over her mind. *I wonder who all these people are? What plans they had before getting stuck here?*

Narrowing her eyes and leaning forward, she studied the man who sat across from her on the other side of the sanctuary. All she could see was his profile—the strong jaw, confident bearing, and elegant clothes. But it was enough. That was Adam Blake. She was sure of it. Don't tell me he got stuck here too, she thought.

She tilted her head to the side and continued watching him. *Maybe he'll look this way. Then I'll wave at him. Maybe he'll recognize me.* But he continued staring straight ahead and finally

Darlene looked away and settled more comfortably in the hard pew.

He probably wouldn't remember her anyway. It had been several years since she'd interviewed him for the local magazine. She remembered well that interview. It had been one of the best ones she'd ever done and had enhanced her reputation with the news editor of the paper. After that the assignments had poured in and she had grabbed every one. Even though Barry hadn't liked her working and wanted her to stay home, to be the perfect little housewife he wanted.

At the thought of her ex-husband, Darlene's stomach hardened. Instinctively, she started grinding her teeth. Then, remembering her dentist's warnings, she made a concerted effort to stop. It wasn't easy with all the troubles Barry was giving her.

Picturing him, she felt her face flush. She wasn't sure if it was caused from the soothing heat emanating from the chapel's furnace or her own anger over how Barry had again beaten her in court. Nor did she care as she shrugged out of her coat and settled it around her.

She picked at the skirt of her red, wool suit and wondered if her choice of clothing color had contributed to her legal defeat. She had worn red because it was supposed to suggest power and success. She smirked. It certainly hadn't done that for her.

As soon as the judge handed down his decision for Barry, the first thing she thought was that her red outfit had affected the old codger just as a scarlet cape did a bull. Red must've made her look unsympathetic and encouraged the male chauvinism that had totally seemed to ignore her concern.

Her lawyer, who she paid a small fortune to, had not agreed with her. "It wasn't the color of your suit Darlene," Russell Burrows explained. He was a square shaped man with a balding, oval head and large, round bifocals. Every time she looked at him, she thought of her second grade lesson on shapes. But he was considered to be a great family law attorney who, if necessary, could even be ruthless in order to win. That reason alone caused her to hire him. That she had seen neither greatness nor ruthlessness in the courtroom infuriated her.

"Well then?" she retorted. "Maybe I lost because you, my great attorney, didn't really fight for me." She knew her voice was rising to a shrieking pitch but she didn't care.

They were standing in the hall outside the courtroom and he took her arm, trying to move her away from the people milling around them. He especially wanted to get her out of the hearing of her ex-husband and his lawyer, who were walking toward the elevator with triumphant smiles on their faces. "You know better than that," he said. "The fact is—and I told you this when you first came to me—that you did not have a strong case."

They were moving now, following far enough behind their opposition to avoid being heard.

"I don't see why not. Barry's behind in his child support. Obviously that's because he doesn't love our children anymore. Now that he has that woman's brat." She took a ragged breath as she watched the elevator door slide closed in front of her husband and his counselor, who were both staring at her from the sanctity of the elevator. "I don't think a man who doesn't support his children should be allowed to see them," she continued self-righteously.

"The judge didn't see it that way."

"Obviously."

A new elevator arrived and they stepped inside. Mercifully, they were the only ones in it. As Russell was reaching for the button, Darlene pushed in front of him and jabbed it, sending it to the lobby four floors down.

"Your husband presented a good reason why he was behind in his child support. His business was down due to this lousy economy. Like so many others."

"I don't believe that."

Her attorney shrugged. "He had proof. His financial records." The elevator stopped and he led her into the lobby.

Far ahead of them, Barry was leaving the courthouse. His head was down as he trudged through the thickly falling snow.

For a moment, as she watched him, Darlene's heart felt as though it would burst. He was still so handsome. And she still cared so much. Then her mouth wrinkled into an angry grimace as she turned to her lawyer. "Well I don't care what that old woman-hating judge said. I am not letting him have my children for Christmas."

Russell gaped at her from behind his big glasses. Worry wrinkled his brow. "Darlene please! Do not do that! You've been given very specific orders. Have Cassandra and Trevor ready to go with him tomorrow evening. Or you're going to be held in more contempt." He gently touched her arm. "I'm warning you. The judge could've thrown you in jail today for defying the visitation orders. If you still do it, next time I have no doubt that he will."

She pulled away from him. "I'll take my chances."

"If you do that," he sighed, "I won't defend you. I can't."

She sneered. "Good! You're fired!" Without giving him another look, she turned and hurried out into the snow. She didn't really need him. Next time she'd defend herself and could probably do it better anyway.

The streets were clogged with snow and she hadn't gotten far before her car, like so many others, stalled. It had sputtered to a stop one block from the chapel.

She had been resigned to being stuck in her cold car when she noticed the chapel's blue lit cross shining a welcome from its roof. Relieved, she left her car, and shuffled toward it as fast as the heavy snow would allow her to move. By the time she arrived at the church door, her feet were frigid and her face sore from the icy snow.

Now, sitting in the warm chapel, Darlene felt like she was at last thawing out. As she allowed her body to relax, the beautiful Christmas music slowly massaged away the tightness that had filled her ever since Barry asked for a divorce two years ago.

She looked at the nativity at the altar. The happy couple, who were Mary and Joseph, made her want to cry. *That was Barry and me. Once* They met on a blind date that she hadn't wanted to go on.

Newly graduated, she thought her journalism degree would immediately get her a great job with a newspaper. But that hadn't happened. Since she'd had to work at something, she took a clerking job in a bookstore. Being around words other people had written was the closest thing to journalism that she could find. There she became best friends with Amber Smith whose art degree hadn't done much for her either.

When Amber's boyfriend needed a date for his cousin who was attending a printer's convention, nothing would do but that it be Darlene. "I really don't want to go," she had said.

"But you have to. Please." Amber's brown eyes, which always reminded Darlene of her cocker spaniel's, were pleading. "Do this for me. Puh-leese!"

She'd given in but not before warning her that she would go home early. But when she met Barry Dexter, all thoughts of leaving left her. He had been drop dead gorgeous. Six foot tall, with the physique of the all-star wrestler he'd been in college, he carried himself with an assurance that Darlene found sexy.

Recalling their first meeting, she smiled gently. He had such gorgeous green eyes and long lashes. His mouth was wide with full lips that, within seconds of seeing them, she knew she wanted to kiss. Before the night was over, he had kissed her while they were dancing and she thought she'd pass out.

Barry was in Darlene's hometown for three days to attend the printer's convention his father, who owned a chain of printing and office supply shops, sent him to. But after meeting Darlene, he skipped the convention and spent every minute with her while she played hooky from the bookstore by telling her manager that she was sick. If they decided to fire her she wouldn't have cared because all she wanted was to be with Barry.

When the convention was over, he called his father and told him that he had the flu and couldn't come home until he was better. That bought them four more days. And by then they were engaged.

Her parents were horrified that she would agree to marry someone she had only known for seven days and who lived five hundred miles away in New Stockford. "You need to at least go there and meet his family," her mother said.

"And see if you'll want to live there," her father added.

I immediately did exactly what they suggested. And I loved both his family and his town. Couldn't wait to move here and become his wife.

Two months from the day they met, she along with her parents and older brother, arrived in New Stockford for her wedding. They never regretted their quick marriage. She frowned. Until two years ago when Barry apparently discovered that he did.

From the beginning, they had been extraordinarily happy newlyweds, giddy with love. Because Barry had a good job working with his father in the Dexter Print Shops, Darlene didn't have to work and could immediately start creating a home for them.

Thanks to Barry's folks, who gave them a down payment as a wedding gift, they bought a house right away. She spent the first year decorating it and planting a beautiful rose garden. She also joined the Junior League and took up golf so she could play with Barry at the country club.

The second year of their marriage, they had Cassandra. They both were so crazy about their baby girl that they could hardly keep from holding and spoiling her. Barry especially had been nuts about her. He used to carry her around in a sling close to his heart and made Darlene keep notes in a little book of ideas they saw at weddings that they might want to use for hers.

Tears drowned her eyes as she wriggled on the hard seat. "Oh Barry," she cried under her raspy breath. "Look what you've done! Now you have another little girl. So you have no time for ours."

"You know that's not true!"

She jerked to attention. *What's that? My conscience?* Pushing back her hair, which was wet and limp on her shoulders, she sniffed. Maybe she had contributed a little to his indifference. But who could blame her? After what he did to her?

She had poured her heart into her marriage. Two years after their daughter was born, they had Trevor. Her son was the spitting image of his Daddy. She chuckled. How the Dexters doted on that boy. Since Barry was the only son, it fell to him to continue the family name. When Trevor was born, that secured it.

Their life fell into a happy, well settled routine with financial security, an active social life and golf games they both enjoyed.

When the children were settled in grammar school, Darlene tried to use her journalism degree. Except for a few published short stories, she hadn't had much luck. Until she started snooping around town, writing human interest pieces, occasional exposes and interviews. At first Barry encouraged her. But as her assignments became more demanding, he urged her to quit.

"You're spending too much time away from the house and kids," he said. Then he kissed her. "We need more of you with us."

But the new recognition that she was getting as a journalist had given her a high as potent as a drug. *I couldn't quit even if I wanted to.* Her lips wrinkled into a sardonic line. *Now it's a good thing I didn't. Thanks to that dead beat Barry, I desperately need the little money I make.*

In spite of their mild disagreements about her working, their relationship had still remained good. Or so she thought until two years ago.

If she could have read the signs then, she would have realized that they were in trouble months before Barry asked for the divorce. He had started working longer hours in the business. She blamed that on his father's sudden death from a heart attack which had created a huge loss for her husband, his two sisters and his mother. And more than an emotional one, it also created a terrible business burden for him. Especially when he discovered the terrible secrets his father was keeping from him and the rest of the family.

Three months after his father's death, when Barry finished reviewing all the books and tax statements with the accountants, he sat down with Darlene and told her his shocking news. "The business is about to go under." His announcement was made without any warm up to cushion the blow.

"I- I don't understand."

"I really don't either. Even now after I've looked at all the finances." He covered his eyes with his hands and shivered. Then he took her into his arms, as if clinging to her would protect him from his world that was falling apart. "It seems that all these years Dad's been gambling heavily. And losing heavily. We're talking really big losses."

The Senior Dexter had mortgaged every one of his six print shops to their maximums. He also made swing loans against his outstanding receivables.

"He'd been struggling just to keep current on all the payments," Barry explained. "But with the down economy, our business fell off. Money became tighter." He shook his head. "If Dad hadn't died when he did, he'd have to face what I am now. That we're so far behind in our bills that we're facing foreclosures and maybe even bankruptcy." He frowned. "That probably would have killed him."

Darlene sat silently and stared at him. She knew her pale face betrayed the shock she felt.

Her husband continued. "Tomorrow I have to tell Mother her house is about to be foreclosed upon." He nodded. "Yes. Dad even mortgaged that."

He had already made arrangements for his mother to live with his older, unmarried sister Dorothy. "Not that I think Mom's going to like it. But she'll have to realize that she doesn't have a choice."

Darlene considered how hard it would be for Mother Dexter and she wanted to cry. But she didn't dare because she knew that if she did, it would make Barry feel even worse.

He took a deep breath before going on. "I've been advised to try to sell off all the stores but the main one. Just for what we owe." He shrugged. "That big chain out west will probably be interested." He sighed. "I sure hope so."

They held each other for several minutes. Finally, Darlene found her voice. "Ah—Honey? What about us?" she asked quietly.

He gave her a tiny, worn smile. "I'll try to keep the main store. It too is mortgaged. And we owe a lot to our suppliers." His shoulders drooped like an old man's. "I've been advised to declare bankruptcy right away. But before I do that, I'm going to try to negotiate with the creditors. Maybe they'll agree to take less instead of getting nothing with a bankruptcy."

In the end, the chain bought the stores and Barry kept the original one his father had started. But the strain on them and their finances took its toll. Gone was their luxurious lifestyle— the country club, kids' private school, and charge cards.

They had even downsized to a smaller house. Her dream house was gone. That hurt her most because she poured so much of herself into it. But she hadn't cared. "We have each other and that's all that matters," she told him.

Then, two years ago on the day after Christmas Barry asked

for a divorce. He had been working long hours and they had seemed to be growing apart because of it. But Darlene simply blamed it on the stress he was under.

She sniffed sarcastically. Little had she known!

The children were visiting his mother at Dorothy's. Darlene didn't realize then that he arranged it so that he could speak to her uninterrupted. They were sitting at the kitchen table, eating tuna fish sandwiches and drinking coffee.

She had expressed delight that he wasn't working at the store. "No kids in the house. And us all alone." She giggled. "I can sure think of something fun for us to do."

He gave her a somber look. "Darlene, I have something to tell you. And I warn you it's going to be hard to hear. Awful really."

She felt her smile disappear as a frown dented her brow. Leaning slightly forward, she realized she was afraid to speak.

Finally, he did. "I don't know how to say this Darlene. And God knows I don't want to hurt you. But—well," he gasped. "I want a divorce."

His words hit her as though they were bullets from a machine gun. She felt her eyes widen and her mouth fall open.

"It's not you," he quickly continued. "It's me. I've just been so unhappy. So miserable."

Her mind had been so numb that she couldn't register all that he was telling her. But later, after he'd taken an already packed bag and hurried from the house, she started to remember his feeble explanation. He felt that if he could free himself of the demands of family life that he might become happy again. Or at least somewhat content.

"Now I'm just so depressed that I'm no good to anyone," he explained. "Least of all you and the kids. You all deserve better than I can give."

She only asked him two questions. "Is there another woman?" was the first one.

He had not hesitated to shake his head. "No."

"Don't you love me anymore?" was the second.

Sighing, he looked at the ceiling before answering. "I can't say I love anyone right now. I'm just so miserable." He promised to continue supporting her and the children

At first when he picked up the kids for a visit, she would try to talk to him. She even cried and begged him to give them another chance. But he always said the same thing. "Not now Darlene." That always gave her hope that one day he would come back.

Then six months after he moved out, when he pulled into the driveway to return Cassandra and Trevor after having them for a week-end, she opened the front door to see a woman sitting in the front seat beside him. When he saw her looking at him, he gave her a guilty smile. As soon as the kids climbed out of the car and slammed the door shut, he gunned the motor and quickly backed out of the driveway.

She tried to keep her voice casual. "Who's the lady with Daddy?"

Cassandra, who had just turned ten and was very close to her father, gave her a haughty glance. "Nobody important."

Darlene turned to her precious little Trevor who adored her. "What about her Trevie?"

He peeked nervously at his sister and rubbed his left shoe against his right leg.

"It's alright Sweetheart," Darlene said. "You can tell Mama." She gave Cassandra a warning look. "In fact you children must never, NEVER keep any secrets from Mama."

Trevor smiled up at her with the countenance of an angel. "She's Daddy's girlfriend Mama." Then his little face fell. "She's going to be our new Mommy."

Darlene couldn't help herself as the tears blasted from her eyes in torrents.

Cassandra glared at her little brother. "You weren't supposed to tell!"

Trevor hugged his mother's leg and started to cry. "I'm sorry Mamma. I didn't mean to make you cry."

She picked him up and cradled him. "Oh Sweetheart you didn't. It's the—the news about Daddy that's making me cry." Then she forced them both to sit with her and tell her everything they knew about Barry's girlfriend.

They just met her that week-end. Her name was Tammy Carter.

"Do you know how long Daddy's known her?" Darlene asked her daughter.

She shrugged. "No."

"What's she like? Is she nice?" As soon as she asked those questions, Darlene regretted them. She shouldn't have shown that she cared because she knew that Cassandra would tell him of her interest.

Trevor sighed. "I guess. She made me cupcakes." He looked down at his shoes and shook his head. "They were pink. I didn't like them as much as I love the brown ones you make."

Cassandra's eyes shone. "She's really fun. She let me put on all her make-up. Even helped me." She frowned. "But Daddy made me wash it off before I came home. He said you wouldn't like it."

"He was right. I wouldn't. You're too young for make-up."

Her daughter threw a defiant look at her. "Tammy doesn't think so."

"Well I do. And even though this—this person might become your other Mommy, let me make one thing very clear. I am your real mother and what I say goes."

Cassandra's eyes narrowed angrily. "Daddy said you'd act like that when you learned about Tammy." She turned her glare onto her brother. "Which is why he didn't want us to tell you."

Prior to that heart wrenching discovery, Darlene had been content to go along with anything Barry suggested regarding their separation and potential divorce because she believed that he would eventually come to his senses and return to her. But the next day Darlene consulted the first of the four lawyers she hired to represent her in what turned out to be an ugly divorce. Because when she learned, from a clerk in his store, that Barry had been cheating on her with Tammy before he left, Darlene pursued justice with an angry vengeance. She fought him over everything. Even when the third attorney, after a year of wrangling over financials, told her that his offers of the house, spousal and child support and medical and life insurance were most generous, she held out for more.

Not until her husband signed over to her all the family burial plots except the one for his mother next to his father would she sign the divorce papers. "What can you possibly want with my family's graves?" he'd asked her. "You hate them now."

She'd given him a wicked smile. "I intend to sell them."

He'd ended up buying them back in order to keep strangers from lying with his parents.

When she did that, her attorney left her. But she didn't care. She got all that she could possibly squeeze out of Barry, including full custody of the children. By then Tammy was pregnant and he had been desperate to get the divorce over with so he could marry again. Otherwise Darlene knew, he would have fought her for joint custody of the kids. As it was, the court gave him two week-ends a month, shared holidays and one month every summer to be with his son and daughter.

Because she was so angry all the time, Darlene's writing suffered and the assignments that had been so plentiful decreased.

Then when it became obvious that the children were happier being with Barry and Tammy, Darlene started finding reasons to keep them from seeing him. When their half sister was born, she accelerated her efforts to stop the visits. The pain she'd felt at their joy when they saw the baby—who Darlene considered that brat -- for the first time still clawed her heart.

Cassandra was actually tingling with pride. "Mama, Tammy

let me give Baby Rose her bottle all by myself. And I even burped her!"

"And I got to hold her," Trevor grinned. "Daddy said she already knows I'm her big brother and she likes me."

Knives slashed Darlene's very soul as she decided that she had to put a stop to those visits. Never would she let that woman steal her children as she had her husband.

When Barry's child support payments started to fall behind, after already getting her spousal support stopped by the courts, she had the perfect excuse to keep the kids from him. "No money no kids," she told him when he called to arrange the children's visits.

He ended up taking her to court where she was ordered to let him see Cassandra and Trevor as the divorce order decreed. But she had held out until today. She felt her face contort into the angry mask that had become her normal appearance.

She didn't need her lawyer to tell her that the judge would arrest her for contempt if she didn't turn the children over to that rat. And she would but not until after Christmas. She had hidden them with one of the few friends she had left, who had done the same thing to her ex-husband that Darlene was doing to Barry. Her fingers curled into tight fists. Tomorrow, when Barry comes to her house for the kids no one would be there. It would be all dark.

She intended to be with her children and her friend, laughing over the trick she played on her ex. *But now maybe I'll be stuck here instead.* Her face softened slightly. *Oh well! It could be worse. At least I'm warm. And this is a pretty little place.*

The music continued to cradle her lovingly and she felt her eyelids start to slide over her eyes when a stern voice suddenly penetrated her soul.

"Darlene you have to let go of this hate! Now!"

Shock stiffened her back as she looked around her. *What is that?* Terror filled her as panic crawled over her entire body.

"It's the voice of God. Your Creator. Who gave you the beautiful children you are destroying."

The knives, that seemed to be always in her heart, slashed deeper. *I love my kids!*

"You do not."

She gasped as her entire body started to shake so hard that the elderly lady sitting near her turned toward her.

Darlene smiled slightly and waved away her concern.

The voice continued speaking to her inner being. "If you loved your children as you say you do, you wouldn't deprive them of their father who loves them. And who they love."

If he loved them he wouldn't have left them. And me

"You have a valid point. What Barry did was wrong. I am totally against the adultery he committed. But that doesn't' change the fact that he is their father. And they need him in their lives. You need him in their lives."

Never! I don't want him in their lives. I don't need it.

"Yes you do. Because only then can you have a life that's free of this hate and evil vengeance. All because he hurt you."

Darlene's head felt like it was being turned by invisible hands to look at the stained glass portrayal of Christ on the cross.

"Darlene, you are as guilty of doing evil as the Romans who killed My Son. Because your hatred for the man you still love is even greater than theirs was for the man they didn't understand."

Tears flowed down her cheeks. *It's true! I do still love Barry. And it hurts me that he's—he's replaced me.*

"I know Dear Child." Now the voice was gentle and soothing. "But if you'll just rid yourself of the hate and replace it with love for Barry and even Tammy and their little Rose, your life will be so much better. Your children will be happy again and love you even more than they ever did. And your heart will be ready to receive a new love."

How can I forgive him? After what he did to me. The betrayal. The hurt.

"My Son was asked that same question when he was living on earth. He told his Disciple Peter that he should forgive someone who sinned against him seventy times seven."

That's a lot.

"It seems so. But may I remind you that My Jesus forgave the very people who crucified him. Just as he does all your sins and Barry's. And everyone else's if they will just accept Him."

She looked at her trembling hands. *I feel so lonely. So unloved.*

"Oh Darlene! I love you. And if I'm for you—no one can be against you. Least of all Barry and Tammy."

Suddenly, her body stopped shaking as it seemed to sink into the pew. Never had she felt such peace as she was experiencing then. *Oh God! I am so tired of fighting. And being angry.*

"Then put those burdens on me. I'll make them light. And give you a peace that passes all understanding."

Deep breaths filled her as her heart seemed to knit. Gone were its painful slashes. And she could feel the deep, angry lines on her face disappearing as joy radiated from her. She looked again at the couple in the nativity.

She no longer fit into that scene because she didn't have a husband anymore. But she did still have that baby in the manger who had become the man on the cross. Her lips lifted into a smile that she was certain lit up the whole room. *With His help, I'll love my children and myself enough to give them back their father.*

CHAPTER 9

◆ ✦ ◆

The Corrupt Politician

Old Ben Dickerson moved slowly to the chapel's front door that opened onto the snowy stoop. His watch read midnight and he wondered if the weather had improved even a little bit. With the organ's Christmas music filling the sanctuary, it had been quite a while since he heard the wind roaring at the windows. *Maybe the snow's slowin' down some. Or stopped altogether.*

Just as he reached the heavy door, it burst open. A large man, built like a professional wrestler, charged into him, hitting Ben's chest so hard that it knocked the wind out of him. Ben grabbed the door to keep from falling. "Hold on there Fella." he gasped. "No need to rush so."

Shivering, the man barely looked at him. "Freezing cold! I need to get warm!"

Old Ben wrinkled his nose and his eyes narrowed. The man's breath reeked of alcohol and his eyes, a dark brown that were almost black, resembled a wild animal's as they flitted from side to side, assessing his surroundings. Ben wasn't sure he wanted this fellow here with the other people.

He tried to touch the man's arm but he yanked it away. "Perhaps you'd like to sit here?" The old caretaker motioned to a chair right beside the door, hoping the smell of him would blow out instead of in.

"No. I'll go in there." The big man nodded toward the doors that led to the sanctuary. "Unless," he added as he thrust his head close to Ben's, "you have some objection." His round face, lined with hard living, resembled an angry bulldog's. "And if you don't like my going in there, you'll be sorry."

For a few seconds the men glared at each other, testing. Old Ben counted off the seconds that ticked in his head. Here was a real bully. He always felt he would give his life for his beloved church. Even told his Nellie that. Now maybe he was being given that opportunity.

He didn't understand the overwhelming feeling of apprehension that he had for the big pushy man. There was something about him that was foreboding. And it had nothing to do with the fact that he obviously had too much to drink. Even though he was a teetotaler himself, he didn't hold others' imbibing against them. No! The man simply didn't belong in the chapel and Ben had to get rid of him.

Old Ben pulled himself up to his tallest height, which was about four inches shorter than the other man.

Suddenly, a voice spoke to his mind. Its tone was commanding. "Step aside. Don't mess with him."

Old Ben relaxed his shoulders, and then moved away. I still better say something, he thought. He forced a smile "Of course you can go inside. It is warmer there. In fact, many people are already there. Each worshipin' the Christ Child in their own way."

At the mention of Jesus, Old Ben noticed the man's entire

posture cringe. Then, without another look at him, the "Bully"—as he had decided to think of him—lumbered into the sanctuary.

———————— ◆ ————————

Homer Henry Hamilton VI took a back pew on the right of the sanctuary. *That bossy old coot who tried to keep me from coming in here was right. The place is warm. Even down right hot.*

Homer shrugged out of his heavy ski jacket and untied the silk scarf around his neck. His throat was dry. Instinctively, he reached for the flask he kept inside his jacket then, discovering it wasn't there, he dropped his hand to his lap. He had been so mad at being stood up that he hadn't thought to take his Scotch with him when he locked the car. He had just wanted to get someplace warm. He looked nervously around him, as though he suspected people could read his mind. *I usually don't drink that much. Just did tonight to keep my insides warm while I waited in the freezing car for that jerk.*

He'd pulled into the driveway of the empty Victorian house across the street from the church and waited for almost five hours for a business associate who was supposed to bring him money. They selected that old house's driveway because it curved completely around the house, offering them a place to meet in the back where no one could see them. But once Homer turned his large car into the driveway's snowdrifts, it stalled after just a few feet.

So I was forced to sit on the side of the house, like a sitting duck, for all to see! Homer had been furious with himself and his car. It had been stupid to think he could drive into a snow packed driveway even with an SUV the carmaker promised could drive through anything. He snorted. *I should sue them for false advertising!*

He figured that his acquaintance—as he would never call

119

him a friend—would see him from the street and not make his mistake of pulling into the driveway. And once their transaction was complete, Homer would insist that he help dig him out of the icy mess. Which he would surely do because that person would realize that Homer and his car should not be seen on DeLancey Street when the snow stopped and people again moved down the busy street. Especially those guys driving the snowplows, he thought. They all knew him from digging him out of his own place. He sighed. It was too late for him to worry about any of that now. Here he was—all because that rotten bum hadn't showed up.

Anger boiled up inside him again and he took deep breaths in order to get control of himself. Even on his best days, he wasn't in good health. With all the stress of today, he felt his heart racing. If he wasn't careful he'd have a heart attack right here. He shrugged. What did it matter? He was ruined now anyway.

He shivered slightly and turned his attention to his surroundings. He'd had few experiences with churches. Two were the Las Vegas chapels where he married those gold diggers. The others all took place in that cold brick building downtown where he had to attend three funerals of city officials. He'd disliked all of those religious establishments. So consequently, he couldn't really judge whether this little one, with its wood paneled walls and stained glass windows, was anything special. He guessed it wasn't. But maybe it had been once. As New Stockford's Mayor, he knew all about this once great and now almost dead street. "The buildings here are ringing DeLancey's death bell," he told himself. "And this little dump is right along with them."

He looked at the people scattered in the pews around him. He didn't recognize anybody. Good! Hopefully none would recognize him. Because he didn't want to have to invent some kind of story to explain why he was here, in this rundown part of town in this shabby little chapel, if anyone had decided to talk to him.

He glanced quickly at the pictures on the walls. Even he, with no religious knowledge, knew they were pictures of that Jesus who those crazy Christians were so obsessed with. A corner of his mouth lifted into a cynical sneer. *How could they be so gullible? So stupid to buy into all that silly stuff about a man rising from the dead after being killed on a cross. Jerks who believe that must also think donkeys fly.*

Then another thought assaulted him and he shook his head. *You of all people should know how stupid people can be. Look at yourself! And the mess you've gotten into. Talk about being a Jerk!* His heart shivered as he shoved the palm of his hand into his forehead to banish the scolding he was giving himself. But it was no use. The memories of his life started bombarding him, like bombs dropping on a city.

From as long as he could remember—probably when he was three—Hamilton Oaks was the foundation of his life. Sprawled over fifteen acres of cherry, apple and oak trees, it was an immense five story estate not unlike the palaces and residences of European royalty. In fact, the second Homer Henry, his great-great-great grandfather who everyone in the family called Two, traveled to England following the end of the Civil War in 1865. His purpose, as he explained it to his young wife, was to "soak up culture".

When he left her to board an English steamship that would take him to Liverpool, she was about to give birth to their first child. That he refused to wait for that event was a point of contention that would last them all their lives.

Recalling the family lore surrounding his early ancestors, "Ham" sighed softly. He preferred to be called the abbreviated version of his last name instead of the family nickname of "Six" which denoted the number of his generation that followed the original Homer. That Homer, who was born in 1777, was the first of their lineage. Now Ham, who was born in 1955, would be the last. Over two hundred thirty years of Homer Henry Hamiltons in New Stockford and they would stop with him. He shrugged.

He no longer cared how mad his father was over that. Like Two, who didn't care when his wife pitched a fit that he was taking off for the high seas, Ham didn't care about his Dad's anger either.

He nodded proudly. Two had fought the war, took a bullet at Gettysburg and come out of the Army a Sergeant. He was a man's man and a magnet for women.

Ham rubbed his wrinkled forehead. *Why couldn't I have turned out like him?*

Once Two arrived in England, the twenty-eight year old made friends with the son of one of Britain's leading exporters. By the time the young man embarked on his return voyage home, he had a contract from that company to be its sole distributor in the entire eastern third of America. Once home, Two scarcely took time to admire his four-month-old son, who had been named Homer Henry III according to his instructions, and create another baby with his wife Ella Louise. Almost immediately he was off again. Traveling by horseback, he set up agents in thirteen eastern states and started instantly to become rich.

Ten years after his visit to England, he built the estate Hamilton Oaks. During those years, Ella Louise grudgingly bore him six children—the original "Three", plus another son who died a day after his birth, followed by four daughters. After the last one, a fragile girl who had chronic breathing problems that would take her life when she was four, Two's wife told him there would be no more activity that would produce more children. Two didn't care. By then he had more "lady friends" than he could handle. But he did maintain his reputation as an honorable family man by building his wife the beautiful home that was the showpiece of the community. That it was also the homage to his massive ego was lost to no one, least of all his wife.

Also at that time, Two took his rightful place as mayor of New Stockford. At the time of his birth in 1837, the first Homer had already founded the town and become its first mayor. What George Washington did for the country, Homer Henry Hamilton

I did for the town. Known as the "Father of New Stockford", One planned and profited from the town's laws, while all the time enjoying the love and support of its citizens, who even installed a life sized statue of him in the middle of the town square. In 1867 at the age of ninety and still leading the town, One finally died. Family stories claim that he expired while visiting one of his many lady friends. No one could ever prove that but the Hamilton men loved to boast about it. Ham's dark eyes danced at the memory of his ancestor and his foot started automatically bouncing to the organ's enthusiastic rendition of Joy To The World.

After watching the town run by a stupid band of middle class clods, Two had taken over as New Stockford's mayor. It had been the same year that he finished building Hamilton Oaks. Ham knew by heart the stories of Two's elaborate party to celebrate his new house and his new position as mayor. It had been the talk of the whole state as well as others around it. It had really marked him as a Class Act.

Ham glanced behind him at Adam Blake, who was sitting with his eyes closed. Satisfied that the only person he recognized in the chapel wouldn't notice him, he moved more comfortably in the pew and looked at his feet, which had stopped stomping when the organ started the more sedate Silent Night.

Two had a great reputation. Except for what Three did to him. Now there was a loser. Makes me look like a winner. The only surviving son of Two and Emily Louise, Three was as opposite from the first two Homers as a person could be. While they were ambitious, smart and energetic, he was lazy, stupid and slow. He had no interest in anything but women and liquor and he courted both with obsessive dedication. When at nineteen, he met a rousing band of gypsies and wed one of their daughters, Two set about to extricate the heir to his vast fortune from what he considered an outlaw cult. It wasn't easy for the determined mayor of New Stockford to do.

The father of the girl, named Sabetha, informed Two that a child was on the way.

"And your son is the culprit," was the angry declaration.

Family memories record that Two looked at Three, raised an inquisitive eyebrow to which Three merely shrugged and nodded. Two came right to the point. "We'll take the child but not your daughter."

"How much will you pay?" asked the father, whose tar colored eyes were gleaming brightly.

A figure was settled upon and Sabetha was settled into the private home of one of Two's lady friends who also was a midwife. According to family legend, Three had wanted to do the right thing and marry her because he really did love her. But Two wouldn't allow it. Just like my old man, Ham thought. Always determined to have his own way.

The baby was born on Three's twentieth birthday. It was a boy, with the black eyes of his gypsy heritage and the large build of his father's family. The birth had been long and hard and resulted in Sabetha's death. When Two turned her body over to be buried in the pauper's cemetery far outside of town, Three snapped.

The next morning they found him hanging from a beam in the stable. So young yet already defeated by life. Ham shivered. He knew that feeling, having thought often about doing what Three did. But he didn't have the guts.

Emily Louise and her daughters welcomed the baby boy, named, of course, Four into their eager arms.

At first Two ignored the child. Or tried to. But Four was everything that his dead father had never been. As soon as he could focus, his black gypsy eyes studied everything and everyone with a wisdom that defied his age. That, along with a powerful physical strength enabled him to walk at nine months, run at ten, climb and jump at eleven and sit upright on a horse at one year. That had so attracted his grandfather that he took over the boy's rearing. "I'm going to make a real man out of this one!" Two promised and so he did. The best schools, private tutors, coaches, and expensive "cultural" trips to foreign courts were all his.

Only thing Four hadn't received was what none of them got either—a faith and the religion that went with it. The reason for that was simple. None of the grandfathers bothered with it or believed in it. The family never stated what the Hamilton wives felt about such a lack. If any had strong feelings about church and God, that knowledge was never shared nor passed down to the descendants.

Ham figured that his grandfathers had thought about religion the same way that he did. All that Jesus stuff was fine for the masses of losers who populated this world. Ham looked around him. Like these poor fools. But it's not relevant to this world and certainly not to him.

In 1915, while America was ferociously fighting in World War I, Four became mayor of New Stockford. His grandfather, who had kept him out of the war, joyfully turned over to him the city's leadership that he had held for forty years. Four, who looked like his gypsy mother, was only thirty when that happened. But he was very mature for his age, having already expanded his grandfather's business and wealth by over three hundred percent. He had also started buying up scores of land close to the city's rustic downtown section. "New Stockford is going to really grow," he explained. "Especially when the war's over. And we need to own as much of it as possible."

Two simply grinned, patted his considerable paunch and puffed on his Havana cigar. "That boy's got cunning gypsy blood feeding his brain," he would often brag.

The only thing Four couldn't do was have a legitimate son. Ham chuckled. *Not that he didn't try. Had two wives in fifteen years. Each one had girls. Three a piece.* But Four didn't remain faithful to either of his wives and married for the third time.

This one birthed a boy who had the black eyes and strong limbs of this father. That baby was Ham's father. They said that Four immediately divorced his mother and took him, who he called Homer Five, to his second wife and ordered her to raise him, which she did happily. Ham's full mouth spread into a proud grin. He had to say one thing for those Hamilton women. They knew their place and obeyed their men. But of course they didn't dare do otherwise.

While Ham loved the stories of his ancestors' lineage, it bothered him when he learned the truth about himself when he was fifteen. "Your Ma's not really your Ma," the son of a servant told him one day after Ham had been particularly obnoxious about his family's wealth and high standing in the town. "You're adopted."

Ham had immediately marched into his father's study, told Homer Five what he had been told and insisted that the servant and his son be fired on the spot. "For telling such a terrible lie!" Ham exclaimed.

His father's black eyes studied him, as though assessing whether or not he was strong enough to learn the truth. Then he spoke. "You might as well know. The kid wasn't lying. All my wives could give me were girls. I found a woman who had a baby she didn't want. It was you."

Ham's face grew chalk white as Homer Five continued.

"Don't look so put out. That woman only birthed you. Your real mother—the one who raised you and loves you—is my wife."

Ham gulped down the nausea that was crawling into his throat and croaked out a comment. "But—but that woman's part of me."

Homer Five waved his big hand at him, slapping the air. "Nonsense! Get that out of your brain. You belong to us. To me. I bought you!" Then he leaned across the desk and glowered at his son. "Don't you ever speak of this again. Ever!" His voice was threatening. "And never let your mother know you know. She's loved you like you're her own. It would kill her if she knew you know the truth."

Ham left his father, went to his room and cried for hours. Then he never spoke or thought of his birth again. Until his father yelled at him when he got his second divorce. By that time Homer Five had become New Stockford's mayor and tripled again the Hamilton family's businesses. "I don't know what's wrong with you Six," Five yelled.

"Ham," his son corrected. "I go by Ham."

"Well whatever you call yourself—you're still a loser!"

Ham thought of what a loser his father was and he had wanted to tell him that. To remind him that he too had not been able to father a son. But when Five proceeded to count on his fingers all that was wrong with him, Ham hadn't had the guts to fight him.

"You can't find a decent woman," the old man yelled. "And when you get any woman—even tramps like you've married—you can't keep 'em. At least long enough to have a child. Even a girl."

"New Stockford is hardly Vegas," Ham offered lamely. He had found, and married, two showgirls in the last seven years. He'd known little about them and suspected that they would find his hometown boring. Yet still he married them. He never could figure out why he practiced such rebellion. Maybe it was the only way he could upset his father. And it worked. He was always mad over them.

His father was continuing to bellow like the old bull Ham thought he was. "It's better than Vegas. The Sin Capital of The World!" It had shocked him that his father had the gall to call a whole town sinful after the lying he and his ancestors had done to acquire so much of New Stockford. But Ham should have known better. By then he knew the truth about all of the Henry Homer Hamiltons who had come before him. Yet he had remained silent, continuing to hang his head like he always did when his father scolded him. "I wish you could find a good woman. Like your mother. And settle down."

At the memory of his mother, a tear escaped the corner of his left eye. He brushed it away. *You've been gone for ten years Mom. And I still miss you as though it was yesterday. You really were the only one who ever loved me.* He glared at the cross at the altar. There couldn't possibly be a good God if his mother was given cancer and allowed to die. He couldn't believe such a thing.

A voice seemed to speak into his head. It sounded like someone was whispering through his teeth. "You're so right about that! The God this church believes in doesn't really exist. It's good that you're too smart to believe those lies!"

Ham's spine quivered as he sat up straighter and looked around him. *Who said that?* No one even looked at him. *I must be going crazy. From all these troubles.*

"No," the voice became a murmur to his heart. "You poor man. You're not crazy. Just tired of the struggle. It's too much for you."

Tears filled Ham's eyes and he pressed his trembling hands over them. *You're right. I am tired. I've nothing to live for.*

"That's right. Not even your own father likes you. But who can blame him? You are such a stupid Jerk. Such a loser. Really worth nothing."

Ham's mind, prompted by the voice in his head, turned back to the memory of his father's anger after his second divorce from the Las Vegas showgirl. "Maybe if you got your nose out of books you could make something of yourself." His father's tone had been thunderous.

"I just finished law school," Ham said. "Like you wanted me to do."

"Yeah," Homer Five had snapped. "But I didn't think it'd take you six years. Most people—smart ones that is—do it in four."

In the end nothing Ham said mattered. He ended it by leaving his father's den and house. They didn't speak for six years.

During that time Ham built a successful practice specializing in corporate and government law. His clients were fortune five hundred companies and large municipalities. And eventually Homer Five realized his son wasn't such a loser after all. They had reconciled on Christmas Day 1989. If one could call speaking to each other during a meal reconciliation. But it had pleased his poor mother greatly and for that Ham had been happy.

After dinner his father invited him into his den and offered him a Havana cigar just like the ones every man in the family had smoked for years.

"No thank you. I don't smoke," Ham said.

"Nonsense! Every man who is a man smokes!"

"Well I'm one who doesn't." Ham cleared his throat and sat forward, as though to spring out of the wing chair that stood before his father's desk. "So what did you want to discuss with me?"

"I've been watching your career." His father took a long pull on the cigar and studied it as though it was a rare artifact. Then he blew his smoke at Ham. "You seem to be doing pretty good."

Pretty good? I'm doing darn good You Old Fraud! Not voicing his thoughts, Ham simply sat quietly and stared at his father as he waited for more of the older man's words.

"You should go into politics. Like all we Hamilton men."

"I don't want to."

Homer Five shook his head and plopped the cigar into an ashtray. "What a dumb thing to say! Why would you say such a thing?"

"Because it's true."

"Why?"

"Why don't I want to go into politics?" Ham gave his father the cynical sneer that he used in court on his opponents. "Obviously I've seen it first hand and not liked it."

The elder Hamilton, who had been lounging in his desk chair, jerked up straight. The chair creaked under his weight. "Look here Boy I've done a lot of good for this town. As have your grandfathers before me."

"The town's also been very good to you. I believe the term is "lining your pockets"?

His father's face was growing bright red. In the six years since he had seen him, Ham noticed that Homer Five's chins had multiplied.

"So I've made a few bucks. That's no crime! All my gains were made honestly."

Yeah. You knew how to manipulate the law. To barely stay within it. To his father he simply said: "The point is I'm not going to follow you into politics."

For eleven years after that conversation, Ham evaded all the grass roots efforts he knew his father was orchestrating behind the scenes to get him into the city's government. Then ten years ago, when a crisis with the school district and ill health brought about his father's retirement Ham relented. He didn't change his mind to please his father. Rather the men who were running for mayor were so flagrantly corrupt that Ham couldn't bear letting one of them run the town. Rather, he did it because he loved New Stockford. He easily won his bid for Homer Five's seat, which his father turned over to him with gloating joy.

For the most part I've served honorably. Didn't use my position for any personal gain. He frowned. *Until now. When I was forced to do something I swore I'd never do.*

"You had no choice," the voice that had spoken to him before said. "You have to save yourself."

Ham nodded. *I am desperate. But—but it's so wrong.*

"No it's not."

"Yes it is!" This voice was different. Calmer than the other, it had an authoritative ring that sounded like it possessed the wisdom of the ages.

The hairs on the back of Ham's neck tickled him. *Who...who are you?*

"It's nothing!" The first voice practically hissed. "Pay no attention to it."

"I am all that is true. And all that is good in the world and in you." The sound of that second voice was like a million bells ringing. It pulled at Ham like a magnet to steel.

Then the first voice interrupted the wonderful attraction. "Don't listen to that. It will just upset you."

Ham was shaking. He didn't understand what was happening. It was like two different people—or beings—were talking in his head. And he didn't know what to do. He cringed at the mess he now found himself in. A mess of his own doing, which had started when he discovered the casinos.

It began innocently enough. No longer interested in finding someone to marry, in spite of his elderly father's constant commands to keep the family alive, he turned in his loneliness to the excitement of gambling. First it had been poker, then Black Jack and Craps. Now it was all of those and the Horses. *I always lose more than I win. Now I'm faced with losing Hamilton Oaks if I don't make good that payment by next week.*

He remembered Old Man Dexter who used to own a bunch of print shops in town. Rumor was that he'd gambled so much money that his family lost almost everything after he died. If that had been a scandal, Ham thought, imagine what it would be if he lost his family's estate! From habit, he hung his head. *What oh what can I do?*

"Go to your father. Confess what you've done. He will understand and help you." The second voice was so convincing that Ham's fear of doing such a difficult thing almost subsided.

Then the other, more familiar voice pulled at him. "Don't be a fool! You can't go to that mean old man. He'll eat you alive!"

Ham felt himself nodding inwardly as he continued to listen.

"Go ahead with your plan. Take that payoff. It's what everybody does for favors."

But—but it's selling out my town.

"So what? Everybody does it. Why should you be any different? Besides nobody will know. You can be rich again in no time."

The authoritative voice was gentle. "What good is it for a man to gain the whole world if he loses his soul?"

Ham put his head in his hands and wept. Then he hurried from the chapel, no longer caring that it was still snowing heavily.

DECEMBER 24

CHAPTER 10

The Christmas Chapel

Old Ben Dickerson opened his eyes, yawned and straightened his stiff body that was slumped in the left pew. Sometime after the Bully Man hurried out of the chapel, Ben had fallen asleep. *Guess it's the warmth and soothing music that knocked me out!* He rubbed his eyes in an effort to awaken his sleepy mind.

As he looked around him at the chapel's visitors, he noted that all were relaxing and many, like he had been, were sleeping. He looked at his watch. Five o'clock in the morning! Christmas Eve had begun.

Quietly, so that he wouldn't disturb his guests, he moved out of the pew and made his way to the lobby. He walked slowly, his arthritic back and knees complaining against the cold weather and stiff pew. He thought of the soft bed in his small apartment at the back of the church and how good it would feel to eventually get into it for a real sleep. As he approached the church's front door, the rumble of engines tickled his ears.

Was that what he thought it was? And what he hoped it was?

He cracked open the door and peeked outside. Then he flung it open and stepped out. The snow had stopped, the stars were twinkling and two huge snowplows were clearing the streets. "Thank you God!" he said to the air around him.

Smiling broadly, he hurried back to the front of the chapel and turned off the Christmas music that had been automatically playing from the organ. At the sudden silence, many people awakened and sat up straighter in their pews.

He took his place in front of the pulpit as he would never presume to stand behind it. Pulpits were only for preachers—which certainly wasn't him.

He cleared his throat and grinned. "Ladies! Gentlemen!" He raised his voice into a shout. "I have wonderful news!"

They were all alert now and leaning forward expectantly.

"The snow has stopped. The snowplows are clearing DeLancey Street!" He nodded enthusiastically. "I 'spect you'll be able to get where you need to be mighty soon now."

Shouts of joy and clapping answered him.

Chuckling, he nodded and held up a hand. "Before you go, I just want say Merry Christmas and Happy New Year. On behalf of this little 'ol church—DeLancey Community."

"Thank you," many cried and they all applauded as he walked down the center aisle toward the lobby. *Those folks sure look happier than when they got here. Maybe their time here helped 'em some.*

He had just propped open the outside door and taken his place beside it when the first of his guests approached him. It was the well dressed man who had arrived looking so frustrated. He reached out his hand and when Ben took it, he held it in a solid grip. "What do you know about that house?" He pointed to the empty Victorian across the street.

Ben sighed. "Miss Emily used to own it. I hear it's goin' to become a glue factory." He shook his head. "Terrible thing to do to that pretty place."

The man smiled. "Don't count on it." Then he hurried down the still snow covered steps.

Next the lady with all the shopping bags approached him, setting one of them down to shake his hand.

He pointed to her packages. "Looks like you're going to have a busy day."

Her thick salt and pepper hair hung loosely as she shook her head. "Not really. My daughter-in-law's bringing dinner."

"Is she a good cook?"

Laughing, she picked up her bag and shrugged. "I don't know. Guess I'll find out tonight."

The disheveled man, who Ben thought looked the saddest of them all, simply nodded as he tried to hurry out of the building.

Old Ben touched his shoulder. "You be careful now."

The man stopped. "I will. I'm starting a new job today." He chuckled. "Guess I better not be late on my first day. Which by the way," he added, "is the Burgers 'N Buns right down the street from you."

"Good!" Old Ben said. "I'll come visit you."

A young woman approached him. During the many hours in the chapel, she sat quietly and seemed to be lost in a deep thought that often made her face both smile and frown.

Ben's eyes twinkled as she offered him a hug and a really big smile. "I hope you have a great Christmas," he said. "And a real good New Year."

She giggled. "Oh I'll have a super New Year! Because I'm going into it single."

He gave her a puzzled look. "If that's what you want Little Lady."

"That is definitely what I want." Her voice lowered as she gave him another broad smile that lit up her round face. "You see I was supposed to get married next week. But I decided not to. Instead," she giggled, "I'm going to stay single. And do what I want to do."

He joined her laughter. "Good for you." He sobered. "I guess."

A pretty woman, who had looked so angry when she came into the chapel, appeared in front of Ben. She wasted no time in getting right to the point. "I'd like to learn more about this church. This street."

Ben looked at her with questioning eyes.

She took his hand and shook it vigorously. "I'm a writer. Maybe I could do an article about this place." She looked around. "It seems to be very old."

"Over a hundred."

Reaching into a large purse, she pulled out a business card and handed it to him. "I'm Darlene Dexter. May I come by after the holidays?"

"Sure. Come anytime. I'm always here."

She started to move away, and then turned back with a smile. "Thank you. For everything. This—this place. It's changed my life."

He tipped his head. "I'm so glad Miss. Jesus is glad too."

Only two people remained. Ben had noticed the old lady and the distinguished looking man hanging back and he wondered why they didn't seem to be in a hurry to leave like the others.

The old woman came up to him. As she stood close to him, he realized with a start that even though she was about his age, she seemed younger. And even pretty.

She held a fat legal envelope in her hand. "Do you run this place?"

"No Ma'am. I'm only the caretaker. The church is run by a Board of Trustees."

"You love this church though. Don't you?"

Smiling, he nodded.

"I could tell." She handed him the envelope. "Here. Take this. Use it for the church. In any way you see fit."

"Why—why thank you Ma'am."

As she stepped outside, he called after her. "Merry Christmas!"

She turned. "It will be. And a happy new year too."

The last guest stood before him. "I couldn't help but hear that the church is in the hands of trustees?"

"Yes Sir. That's right."

"What do they plan to do with it?"

"I'm not sure." Ben sighed. "I 'spect they'll sell it to some developer, who'll tear it down."

The man took a small notebook and pen out of his suit coat. "Would you mind giving me their name and telephone number?"

Ben quickly gave it to him. He'd been with the trustees so long that he knew their information by heart.

"Thank you," the man said as he handed him his card. "I'll be seeing you again. Soon!"

Old Ben watched him leave, then closed and locked the front door.

He moved slowly back to the sanctuary, but before he turned out the lights he sat in the front pew closest to the nativity set at the altar.

"Well 'lil Jesus, what did you think of our company? Did you talk to 'em? Touch their hearts like you did those shepherds and wise men a long time ago?"

The figure of the baby in the manger seemed to smile at him and Ben rubbed his eyes. "I'm so tired I'm seein' things," he told himself. Yet he continued to sit there, not wanting to leave the warmth of the sanctuary and the love that the nativity and the pictures of Christ represented.

His mind turned back to his guests, as he thought of the people who had sought refuge there. They were a varied lot and as each of their faces entered his mind, he spoke to the baby in the manger.

"Remember that worn out woman with all those packages 'lil Jesus? She sure left happier than when she came in. Bet you had a lot to do with that."

"Isn't it good that pretty girl's not goin' to get married? Guess so or you wouldn't let her change her mind. Now I'm wonderin' what you got up your sleeve for her."

"And that fancy dressed man who asked about Miss Emily's house that the glue factory people want. I saw him go across the street to see it. Wonder why he did that?" He chuckled. "Guess you know."

"That man with the new job. Be with him 'lil Jesus. Help him to do good with it. And be happy. He seemed so sad."

"And that writer lady. She wants to write about us. Now what do you think of that? And what she said 'bout her life having been changed here." He chuckled. "Guess you know all about that too."

As he thought about each of their visitors, he suddenly remembered the old woman. He reached inside his jacket pocket and took out the thick envelope that she had given him. "Now this is odd. She gave me this for the church."

He stared at the envelope and looked at the manger. "Should I open it?"

Since no verbal answer actually came to him, he felt it would be all right to at least take a little peek.

He gasped when he saw its contents. "Money 'lil Jesus! Lots of it!" He sighed. "The trustee's will sure like this." Then he frowned. "But will they fix the church with it? 'Cause lots needs to be done. A new roof. Better heating and carpeting."

He counted the bills. "Fifty thousand dollars! A fortune! I'm scared to have it here. I need to get it to the trustees right away. But how?"

Suddenly the last guest's face flashed across his mind. That man had given Ben his card after getting the trustees' contact information.

He reached into his pocket and pulled it out. "Pastor William Worth," it read.

"Lil Jesus, do you know what this is about?" He smiled. "Of course you do. You know everything."

He looked again at the money, which he had returned to the envelope. "Maybe I'll keep this til after that Pastor talks to the trustees. He said he'd see me again. And that might change how they'd use this money. Think that'd be okay?"

He stood and stretched. "I'm dog tired. Gonna take a good long nap. Might not even wake up 'til its time for me to come back here to wish you a Happy Birthday."

He walked slowly to the figure of the baby in the manger and knelt down beside it. He reached for one of the baby's hands that was lifted toward heaven and caressed it. "Thank you. For comin' down here so long ago. To save us from our sins so we can live forever. And also thank you for bringin' those special folks here to spend some time with us." His eyes twinkled. "I 'spect you even worked some of your miracles on 'em."

Then he recalled the man he'd called The Bully who had almost knocked him over when he ran in and then, after only a little while in the chapel, hurried out as though something was chasing him. He cringed. "That man's got the most troubles of all lil' Jesus. And only you can fix him. But somehow," he shook his gray head, "you're gonna have you a big job with that one."

He patted the baby's face with gentle fingertips and offered a small smile to the infant that seemed so real to him. "You know I'm just a simple man. Don't understand how you work. I just know you do. You care about all of us. Even that Bully Man and Old Ben here. So I just want you to know I love you. And appreciate you"

Struggling to his feet, he looked down at the baby as tears started to fill his eyes.

"One more thing 'lil Jesus. If you don't mind. When you see my Nellie, please tell her I love her too. Okay?"

DO YOU WONDER WHAT
HAPPENS TO THE VISITORS
OF
THE CHRISTMAS CHAPEL
AFTER GOD CHANGES THEIR HEARTS?

CHECK OUT THE NEXT BOOK
IN
THE DeLANCEY STREET CHRONICLES:
TURMOIL ON DeLANCEY STREET
DUE OUT EARLY SPRING 2014

DO YOU WONDER WHY THERE WILL NEVER
BE PEACE IN THE MIDDLE EAST?
BARBARA'S NOVEL ABOUT
THE PATRIARCH ABRAHAM, (AS TOLD
IN THE BOOK OF GENESIS)

HEIRS OF ABRAHAM attempts to explain this.
It covers a span of four thousand years, from ancient Mesopotamia and Egypt as well as modern Israel. It deals with a real man's struggles with faith, power, love and cowardice, his women, Sarah his wife and Hagar his slave, and their two sons—Ishmael and Isaac, whose descendants have fought forever for the land now known as The State of Israel.

HEIRS OF ABRAHAM IS AVAILABLE NOW ON
THE WESTBOW WEBSITE, AMAZON AND ALL
PLACES WHERE GOOD BOOKS ARE SOLD.

FOLLOW BARBARA ON HER WESTBOW
WEBSITE; FACEBOOK
OR EMAIL HER: bjwitcher@cox.net

Reader's Guide

1. How would you describe "Old Ben" Dickerson? As someone you would like to know, wouldn't even notice or avoid at all costs?

2. When he opens the closed chapel and turns on the heat and electricity, he appears to be ignoring the trustees' wishes to control expenses by keeping it closed. Does this mean he defies authority or is there another reason for his actions?

3. When businessman Adam Blake entered the chapel, how does he show the kind of person he is? Is he someone you would like to know?

4. Knowing about his tragic childhood, can you blame Adam for doing what he did, which includes disowning his brother Joey and stealing from his mentor, in order to be rich, successful and powerful?

5. If you were confronted by God as Adam was, how would you respond?

6. Do you believe Adam will really change?

7. Have you ever been as heartbroken as Elizabeth Curtis?

8. Is she just a coward or a genuinely grieving woman whose dependency on her husband left her totally lost?

9. Do you accept God's explanation for why He sometimes allows people, such as Big Jim, to go to Him?

10. Why do you think she gave Old Ben her savings for the church? Was she being irresponsible or suddenly grateful for her "new lease on life"?

11. Why is Pastor Will Worth unhappy and even indifferent when it seems that he has everything any pastor would want—including fame?

12. Like so many successful, busy couples he and his wife Becky have grown apart. Is this particularly dangerous for pastors?

13. When God confronts him, Will gets defensive instead of immediately listening to the God he professes to serve. Why is this?

14. Do you believe he will follow through on taking over the little chapel and leaving his mega church—particularly when he returns to it and realizes what he is giving up?

15. Young Susie Porter has been a "people pleaser" all her life as she lived in her more glamorous sister's shadow. How

did that contribute to her disastrous relationship with Frank Mercer?

16. Is she right in cancelling her wedding and will she go through with it when she gets back with her family?

17. In the silence of the chapel, what does Jesus tell her about His own life that gives her courage to risk angering her parents to live the life she wants?

18. Like so many people in today's tough economy, Brett Montgomery lost his high-paying job, hasn't been able to find another and now faces trouble in his marriage. How are both Brett and his wife Diana contributing to their problems?

19. What is really behind Brett's anger at having to accept the minimum wage job cooking hamburgers at the Burgers 'N Buns?

20. God gives his attitude some serious adjustments! Do you think it will take?

21. Isabelle Franklin gave up her own dreams to be a super mom and wife. Now she's bitter. What happened?

22. She spared no time, money or energy in helping her children excel in their interests. But did she really do that for them or herself?

23. All of her relationships, including the one with her husband, are falling apart. What does God tell her about this?

24. Do you think she'll really change her controlling ways?

25. When her husband left her, Darlene Dexter's life was shattered. Can you blame her for being angry and vengeful, particularly since he isn't paying child support so that he can afford his new family?

26. How does God turn her around and will it really work?

27. It seems that the town of New Stockford has been controlled by a family of men since its creation and they've all been corrupt. Now the sixth Mayor Homer Hamilton has come into the chapel because a developer who was supposed to give him a bribe for a favor doesn't show up. His life, thanks to compulsive gambling, is in total ruin and as he considers what to do, he faces two alternatives. What are they and who brings them?

28. When everyone leaves the chapel, do you think Old Ben and the little church will remain the same?

29. Thinking of the chapel's eight stained glass windows portraying Christ's life, which one most represents your life?

30. Which visitor to the chapel can you most identify with?

Made in the USA
San Bernardino, CA
07 December 2015